WE ARE THE GOLDENS

ALSO BY DANA REINHARDT

The Summer I Learned to Fly

The Things a Brother Knows

How to Build a House

Harmless

A Brief Chapter in My Impossible Life

WE ARE THE GOLDENS

DANA REINHARDT

Text copyright © 2014 by Dana Reinhardt
Jacket photograph © 2014 by Shutterstock

All rights reserved. Published in the United States by Wendy Lamb Books, an imprint of Random House Children's Books, a division of Random House LLC, a Penguin Random House Company, New York.

Wendy Lamb Books and the colophon are trademarks of Random House LLC.

Visit us on the Web! randomhouse.com/teens

Educators and librarians, for a variety of teaching tools, visit us at RHTeachersLibrarians.com

Library of Congress Cataloging-in-Publication Data
Reinhardt, Dana.
We are the Goldens / Dana Reinhardt. — First edition.
pages cm
Summary: "Since their parents' divorce when they were young, Nell and her sister Layla have been each other's stability and support. When Layla starts to pull away, Nell discovers a secret: Layla is involved with one of their teachers. Nell struggles with what to do"—Provided by publisher.
ISBN 978-0-385-74257-3 (trade) — ISBN 978-0-375-99065-6 (lib. bdg.)
— ISBN 978-0-385-74258-0 (pbk.) — ISBN 978-0-307-97581-2 (ebook)
[1. Sisters—Fiction. 2. Divorce—Fiction. 3. Teacher-student relationships—Fiction. 4. Sexual abuse—Fiction. 5. High schools—Fiction. 6. Schools—Fiction.] I. Title.
PZ7.R2758We 2014
[Fic]—dc23
2013023351

The text of this book is set in 12.5-point Columbus.

Book design by Heather Kelly

Printed in the United States of America

10 9 8 7 6 5 4 3 2 1

First Edition

For Chelsea Hadley, who is like,
and indeed by marriage is, a sister to me

THERE'S SOMETHING I NEED to tell you.

Don't be mad.

Please. Please don't be mad. I hate it when you're mad at me.

Have you ever woken in the middle of the night, and for just a second you don't know where you are, or the shape of the room, or if you even belong in this world? Yes. I know you have because we used to share a bedroom, and I've heard the sharp intake of your breath. The scrambling through tangled sheets. The blind searching until you realize you're home, in your own bed, and that you're you.

Well, that's the sort of feeling I get when you're mad at me, but it lasts for much longer than a breath and a scramble through sheets; it lasts until I know you're not mad anymore. When things are right between us, that's when I feel like me.

It's always been this way; we know the family joke. When I first learned to talk I called myself Nellayla.

Nellayla.

You were so much a part of me I thought we shared a name until you told me: "I am Layla," and you tapped your chest, then reached out to touch mine. "You are Nell."

I'm sure this rattled my tiny universe. Swept the ground right out from beneath my chubby, uncertain legs. I know this because it's how I feel now when you have to spell out the ways we're not the same.

What divides us is clear to the world around us but has always been murky to me.

Nellayla. The family joke. One of the only things the four of us can still laugh about together.

But is it funny?

Or do I laugh because that's what you taught me to do?

I COUNTED ON THIS BEING the best year of my life. I say this even though I know it's foolish to count on anything, that all sorts of stuff happens we never see coming.

I never imagined Mom and Dad would divorce when I was five. Or that we'd give up dolls, or that you'd want to sleep in your own room, or that I'd have bigger boobs than you. I never imagined that boys as beautiful and perfect as Parker and Duncan Creed could die, but they did, and their parents sold their house and we never spent Christmas there again.

Still, even though I knew better, there were things I looked forward to, hoped for. I believed my freshman year at City Day would kick some serious ass.

My last two years at Pine Academy were fine. I'd been there since kindergarten, and of course I had Felix, but I couldn't wait to start City Day and be Layla's little sister again.

You know all those movies where the kids go to their first day of high school? They walk down the hall and people stare at them, or don't stare, which is sort of worse. Or maybe they wear the wrong clothes, say dumb things, choose the worst place to sit at lunch, and so they become the target of the unspeakably evil cool kids. Etc. Etc. Cliché, cliché.

Yeah, well, those movies always seemed pretty fake to me. The villains and the heroes too simple and obvious when there's probably a little of both in every one of us. And also: none of the kids in those movies had an older sister like you.

Mom dropped us off that morning. Remember? You wanted to drive. Mom said that even if she didn't need her car to get to work, and even if she was crazy enough to lend it to someone whose license was still wet with ink, where on earth would you park it?

That's Mom. *The Fun Killer.*

If we'd been with Dad the night before that first day, he'd probably have given us the keys to his convertible, and donuts for breakfast.

That's Dad. *The Fungineer.*

Heroes and villains. It's not that simple.

Felix was waiting out front on the sidewalk. I knew it was Felix, even though he wore a flat-brim baseball cap, the kind he mocked. I'd know Felix if I woke in the middle of the night not sure where or who I was.

"Hello, lovely ladies." He tipped his ridiculous hat.

You gave him a quick hug and he blushed. You did this because you know that beneath his cool exterior he burns for you with the intensity of a thousand white-hot suns, to quote some Shakespeare.

This should bother me, but come on. How could Felix not harbor a passion for you? You're Layla. Beautiful and brilliant and kind and funny with a good head on your shoulders.

That's what everyone always says: *Layla has a good head on her shoulders.*

Mom and Dad. Gramma and Gramps. Your first-grade teacher even wrote it on your report card.

I used to think this referred to your actual head and its auburn curls. I'd look in the mirror—why wasn't *my* head good on *my* shoulders? Hair too stick-straight? Too many freckles?

Of course, I now know having a good head on your shoulders means that someone is careful, cautious, makes good decisions, and knows right from wrong. Once, this was true of you.

I knew City Day. You'd been there for two years, and sometimes I got to join you at school. The community potluck. The musical your freshman year, when you worked on the lighting crew. The student art open house in the spring, where I ate cold Brie on stale crackers while you showed us your self-portrait in charcoal. A face I knew better than my own stared back with sorrowful, faraway eyes. The next spring you molded your torso in clay. Stunning, but a little too generous in the breast department if you'd asked me, and too skimpy in the waist. It made Dad blush.

I wondered if that was who you wished you were and how you could ever want to be anything other than who you are. I look back and I can see how much you put into your art, how hard you tried, how deeply you felt, and now I know why.

But I didn't see it then.

Maybe you didn't either.

And of course, there was soccer. I only missed your games if I had to play with my team. Standing on the sidelines and shouting "Go, Lightning!" and wearing my purple and gray City Day beanie made me feel part of the school. I could see a flickering image of a future me, the only freshman on the varsity team, warming up the bench.

Hey. This was *my* fantasy, so why wasn't I sprinting downfield to score the winning goal with a perfect high-to-the-right-corner left-footed kick? Because I'm a realist. I try not to waste my time imagining impossible things.

But I did dream of making the team, and that didn't feel so out of reach because I've always been a damn good player—the leading scorer on the eighth-grade team, co-captain, MVP—and you've been talking me up to the coach since you made varsity your sophomore year. Coach Jarvis loves you. So why wouldn't she want another—younger—version of you on the team?

That first day you left me in the hallway to head upstairs to your first class—US History, I'd already memorized your schedule—and said, "Don't forget about tryouts today."

I laughed. Forget?

"So that's who you've decided to be," Felix said to me as he watched you walk away. "The jock? The sporty type? Didn't you get the memo that this is a hipster-urban high school? We're supposed to go gender-bendy and write ironic poetry and whatever. We're not supposed to try out for organized sports."

"I'm not a jock, per se," I said, though explaining myself to Felix felt like a waste of precious people-watching minutes. "I'm just good at soccer."

"First of all, don't say *per se*. And second, I'm good at math. Do you see me signing up for the math club? No. Because I will not be pigeonholed as the math nerd."

See? Even Felix, one of the smartest people I know, believes those stupid movies about high school.

"You're unpigeonholeable, Felix," I said. "Just look at your stupid hat. I'd never have pegged you for a fashion slut."

We stood in the hallway and compared schedules. We had only one class together. Spanish I. Spanish is my Achilles' heel and Felix's native tongue. He declined to point this out when he registered for classes because he's an evil genius, and he figured why not get one free pass in a school as academically rigorous as City Day? And whoever makes the schedules didn't question why Felix De La Cruz was in Spanish I, because that sort of assumption is verboten in politically correct City Day.

A win for Felix, and a win for me, because I had every intention of making him do my homework.

We walked together to freshman orientation in the gym. It felt good to have someone to sit next to, someone to be seen with, because most people didn't yet know that I was Layla Golden's little sister.

I recognized some faces. There were two other kids from Pine Academy, but neither of them were friends of ours. There were some girls I knew from the soccer field and there was Hugh Feldman, the son of a colleague of Dad's, who he tried to force-friend on me when we were in second grade. Remember? It backfired because Hugh pulled down his pants when they came over for brunch and Dad freaked out. So ridiculous. Who cares if you wear pants or not in second grade?

I stared at Hugh Feldman across the gym and imagined him pulling down his pants right then, in the middle of freshman orientation, and it made me giggle. Felix whispered, "What's so funny?" but I didn't tell him because I didn't want him to think I was a big perv.

My classes were okay. I liked English the best, obviously. The syllabus surprised me. We'd be reading books that I knew had things like sex and drugs and bad language, and that was when it first hit me that I was in high school. There would be freedom. There would be choices. There would be blurred boundaries. You know this because you're over halfway done here, but I'm wondering now if it's a mistake, if maybe we shouldn't be expected to find our own way, or put away childish things. Maybe we still need someone to hold our hand.

I looked for you at lunch. No luck. I sat with Marina Baker, whose team we beat 2 to 1 in the finals last season. She's good, but honestly, I wasn't too worried about her when it came to the varsity benchwarming spot with my name on it.

I thought about Parker and Duncan Creed, those poor dead brothers. Sometimes I found myself talking to them, like how when I was younger I used to talk to my stuffed animals. That first day I imagined them seated across the cafeteria, waving me over, gesturing to the empty chair at their table. *Sit with us,* they'd say. Whenever I thought about high school, I pictured beautiful, perfect boys like them. Not the acne-prone, greasy-haired boys with humongous Adam's apples who filled the seats around me.

Anyway, I know I'm going on and on, but it just feels good to go back and remember a time when I still thought I was starting what would be the best year of my life. When there were all kinds of possibilities, plans, things to count on.

But now life has killed the dream I dreamed, or whatever that line is from *Les Misérables,* the musical I sat through three nights in a row just because you were in charge of turning on and off the lights.

I MADE THE TEAM.

I'll probably never know if I made it because I'm your sister or because Coach Jarvis saw my potential, but I don't really care.

I know I'm supposed to want to be judged for who I am and what I can do, but I've never minded being judged for you.

Everyone was really nice to me at tryouts. They know me from my sideline cheering and from pizza parties at Dad's. They joked about what should be printed on the back of my jersey. Little Golden? Golden #2?

Felix watched from the bleachers. He said he'd decided to walk home through the park and stumbled upon us in our purple and gray sweats, but I knew he was worried about me. He understood I'd take it hard if I didn't make the cut.

But also, I knew he liked watching you. And the other girls on the team.

Coach Jarvis didn't post the results until the next day, but as I sat on the grass unlacing my cleats and slipping off my shin guards, she said, "Nice work out there, N. Golden," and I knew that meant *Go home, relax, you have nothing to worry about.*

N. Golden. That's what it says on my jersey. Does yours say *L. Golden?* No, it does not. We both know that you are The Original Golden. You don't need a qualifier.

Mom and Dad fought hard for you. They didn't meet until they were in their midthirties, and then for years they enjoyed their lives as a cohabitating couple with lots of pocket change. They had successful careers and took fancy vacations. They lavished attention on their Bernese mountain dog, who perished, thankfully, before I joined the family because as you know, I'm terrified of dogs, especially big ones.

As Mom approached the big 4-0 it struck them that they might like to have a baby. That's how Gramma tells it. She makes it sound like they were characters in a cartoon comic strip who one day realize what every reader knew all along. Thought balloon: BABY.

So: Quick trip to City Hall. Sad little bouquet of white Gerbera daisies. Wedding lunch at Zuni Café. Then years spent trying to get pregnant. Doctors. Tests. Pills. Hormone shots. Dad depositing his contribution into a little plastic cup, but God knows neither of us wants to think about that, so let's forget I said anything. Several rounds of IVF and voilà: The Original Golden.

Perfect Baby Layla.

Damn if your pictures aren't cute. So smiley and round and wide-eyed. If Mom and Dad had less class, they'd probably have pimped you out to sell teething biscuits or wet wipes. They say you hardly cried, and I don't think parents lie about that sort of thing. You slept through the night at four weeks.

Finally, they had it all.

And then, eight months later: surprise.

Sometimes I think you willed me into existence. Took a look around and thought *I don't want to do this on my own. I need backup.*

Mom and Dad were shocked. At forty-four she was pregnant again, the good old-fashioned way.

Nobody wants to think too hard about his or her conception, but I've always taken a weird pride in how I was made. I like to think I was ushered in by fate. The universe saying: *Uh-uh. That Original Golden needs a little sister.*

Suddenly the perfect child had to be scolded regularly: *Careful with the baby. Don't squeeze her so hard. You're going to suffocate her. Give her some space.*

Our nannies, and there were many who came and went in those early years, liked to dress us up to match. Those are my favorite pictures of us. Especially the one where we're both in purple dresses and I'm wearing my favorite bunny-ear hat and you're wearing a headband with a big purple flower on it, almost as big as your face. You're the awkward-looking one while I shine.

Mom and Dad sent you to kindergarten even though

you'd be the youngest in your class. You were so bright, so eager, so ready.

They decided to hold me back. I don't think this had anything to do with how ready I seemed. I'm pretty sure I could have mastered the art of cutting and gluing and circle time with the rest of the five-year-olds.

Maybe they wanted to preserve my baby-ness for as long as they could. Without a baby, what did they both need to stick around for? I don't think it's a coincidence that Dad moved out the December after I started school.

Who moves out in December? Who doesn't at least wait until after Christmas? He could have done it the week after New Year's. Wouldn't that have been a better time to break up the family? They called a family meeting. They sat facing us in separate chairs; we sat together on the couch. They said they loved us more than anything, and the whole time you kept your arm around me, and I don't remember much beyond the feeling of your palm *tap-tap-tap*ping my shoulder. They said we'd always be a family, the Goldens, that wouldn't change.

The four of us haven't had another meeting since.

Anyway, what I really want to talk about is the other reason I think they had me wait to start kindergarten: they wanted to give us more room to find our own way. I'm sure their shelves full of child-rearing books urged them to foster our individuality, put some space between siblings. And I'm sure they thought they were doing the right thing, because Mom and Dad are genuinely decent people. But they screwed that one up royally.

See, we aren't your average siblings. Those books don't know that I am me and you are you, and yet, we should be near each other.

And maybe, just maybe, if Mom and Dad hadn't listened to those books and held me back, if I'd started at City Day the year before, a freshman to your sophomore, if I'd been nearer, then none of this ever would have happened.

HOW IS IT POSSIBLE THAT you never mentioned Sam Fitz-payne? In all of our conversations about City Day, when I'd sit on your bed until you yawned and told me to get lost so you could get your beauty sleep, and I'd shuffle back to the room I never wanted, how did you never mention him?

He's like Parker and Duncan Creed—the perfect boy I imagined I'd see everywhere, but there were none until the Thursday I saw Sam.

I spotted him in the hall. I noticed the way he circled you.

He's so beautiful. How can you not love that shy smile, the dimple on his left cheek, the shaggy hair, his green-gold eyes? How could you have failed to mention him? How could you not stand still and let him stop circling?

That Thursday after school, as we walked from practice to the bus stop, I said, "Tell me about Sam Fitzpayne."

You stopped and looked at me. "Sam? Really?"

You made a show of thinking it over, as if contemplating him for the first time.

"He's just a boy." You continued walking. "He's a little boy."

Every now and then you exhibit a blind spot. For the most part, you have perfect taste. You look great without seeming to put in any effort. Your room is DIY mixed with classic teen and vintage hip. As for music—everything I listen to I chose because you liked it first.

Anyway, about Sam. It was really hot on the bus ride home. That's September in San Francisco. Summer finally arrives when there are no free days to enjoy it. I was sweaty and sore and irritated at you. Why? Because sometimes you fail to see gifts dropped right at your feet. You step over them and walk on.

We hopped off the bus a few stops early so we could pick up dinner on Chestnut Street. I like to cook; you don't. You wanted sushi, but I convinced you we should go to Lucca Delicatessen and get ingredients for a spaghetti puttanesca, one of my best dishes. We paid with Mom's credit card.

She was out that night. A date with Barry, probably. She really liked Barry, and we did too, though we teased her that she couldn't possibly marry someone named Barry.

Barry, will you pass the salt?

Barry, what time will you be home?

Barry, don't forget to pick up the dry cleaning.

Who could go through life like that?

This was endlessly funny to all three of us. Poor Barry. He didn't stand a chance.

I feel bad that Mom hasn't remarried. She wants to, and I know that the reason she hasn't has something to do with us. It's not like we've tried to sabotage any of her relationships; it's just that even though we spend three out of every seven days with Dad, we take up a lot of space. Mom is tirelessly devoted to us. We are her north, her south, her east, her west, to quote that W. H. Auden poem. I know it's about a death, but to Mom we're her compass, even if sometimes that's not how it feels.

I think you can be too hard on her. I've never said that because I'm genetically programmed to take your side, but honestly, you could cut her some slack.

We ate our dinner—one of my better efforts. I started clearing the dishes even though I think it should be the job of the one who didn't cook to clean up. I was at the sink, wrist deep in lukewarm water, when you said: "So . . . there's going to be this party Saturday night."

I remember where I was standing because that's what happens when big moments strike: people remember exactly where they were, like they remember exactly what they wore, which in my case was still my sweaty practice gear.

I'm not trying to compare the moment I knew I'd be going to my first high school party to landing a man on the moon or anything, I'm just saying that this was a monumental moment for me and I couldn't understand why you didn't seem to share my excitement.

I looked at you. "Great! I'm in!"

"It's probably going to be lame."

"So? I can do lame," I said. "I can totally do lame."

"Didn't Dad say something about taking us to the movies?"

"Screw Dad."

"Nell. Gross."

"Geez. You know what I meant. He can find someone else to go to the movies with. Like his wife."

"I don't know. . . ."

"Well, I do. We're going to the party."

Dad took the news pretty well. He and Sonia opted for *Citizen Kane* at the Castro since we have a thing against old black-and-white movies. This makes Dad nuts. He sees it as a major failure as a parent that he hasn't nurtured in us a love for ancient cinema. But we just don't like stories that don't relate in any way to the lives we live now.

"Who is hosting this party?" Dad put air quotes around the word *party*.

"A senior," you said, putting air quotes around the word *senior*.

"A senior?" Dad looked over at me. "Does this nameless senior know that there's a freshman crashing the party?"

"Nice one, Dad," I said. "Way to make me feel secure."

You stated the obvious: "Nell's not just *any* freshman."

"No," he said. "She's not. But she's still three years younger than the seniors who'll be there."

"Not technically," I said. "Remember? You made me wait to start kindergarten until I was six?"

"Right," he said, as if I hadn't brought that up one zillion times. "Okay. Here's how it's going to be. You may go to this *party*, but you will be home no later than eleven-thirty, and you will call me if you need a ride, and, Layla, you will keep both eyes on your sister at all times." He pointed to his eyes and then at me.

"Aye-aye, Captain." You saluted him.

Funny. He thought *I* was the one who needed looking after. *You* were the one he trusted.

We walked to the party. Hazel Porter lived on one of those *OH MY GOD* hills a half mile from Dad and Sonia's place in Noe Valley. Half a mile is nothing for athletes like us, unless the last few blocks of that half mile are straight up an *OH MY GOD* hill.

"Feel the burn," you said, huffing and puffing.

"This better reap rewards in my butt, like, immediately."

"Your butt is perfect! It's a work of art!"

"Whatever."

You stopped and turned to face me, and it gave me a sudden feeling of vertigo, like you might tip forward and I'd tip back and we'd both go tumbling down the hill.

"Nell. Don't you know how great your body is? You have a fantastic body. And you're beautiful. You need to know that."

How'd everything turn so serious? I thought we were joking.

"Look," you said, starting up the hill again more slowly. "I don't want you getting insecure or filled with doubt about yourself. Boys have a way of doing that to girls. Of making them feel like they're not good enough. Maybe it's not even the boys, maybe it's the other girls, I don't know. It's just that . . . all this messed-up stuff happens in high school and you have to stay out of it, or rise above it somehow."

"I'm fine with myself," I lied.

"Good, because you should be."

I didn't even know who Hazel Porter was until I saw her in the kitchen by the keg, and then I recognized her as the girl we'd seen walking down the front steps while Felix and I were sitting on the wall outside school, and he looked up and said, in a moment of rare inarticulateness: "Whoa."

I pulled out my phone and snapped a picture of her on the sly. I texted it to him with: *guess where I am*

He texted back: *brag much?*

I was the only freshman at the party, but I didn't feel like Cinderella at the ball; I felt more like the mouse in those books Mom used to read to us when we were kids. Remember? He lived in this grand house where there were lots of fancy parties and he'd dress up and come out of his little mouse hole and he'd mill around and sip champagne and nibble on cheese scraps, completely unobserved by the humans around him.

I felt completely unobserved. Except by you. True to your word, you kept your eyes on me.

It was awesome. There I was, a fly on the wall. I had a Golden ticket—ha, ha. Any freshman at City Day would have traded places with me in a heartbeat.

I hung out on the fringes of your conversations. You seemed bored, like you'd rather be sitting in the Castro with

Dad and Sonia watching some movie about an old guy and his sled. It was the first party of the year. How could you have already been so weary?

Did you even notice him? He started out on the other side of the living room, circled the couch, and pretended to be interested in the bookshelf. He wandered over to the stereo and made an imperceptible adjustment to the volume. Circled back to where we stood.

Sam Fitzpayne.

He waited it out for a song and a half. You didn't even glance in his direction. Then, finally, he turned to me.

"Hi. I'm Sam."

The mouse in that story would have dropped his champagne glass and his scrap of cheese and hightailed it for his mouse hole. I get that mouse, I do, because every impulse inside me screamed: *RUN!*

"Nell," I said. "Nell *Golden.*"

"Ah." He nodded. "The younger sister."

I willed myself not to, but I blushed, as if he'd just paid me a compliment.

We talked, leaning in close so the music didn't drown us out. I told him I'd made varsity soccer because it was the only thing I could think of that might impress him.

I only had half his attention, or less, but still, it was exhilarating. I forgave him the furtive glances in your direction. How he waited to jump ship from me to you.

Finally, you turned to us. "Hey, Sam. I see you've met Nell."

"I have." He looked at me and smiled that gorgeous smile.

"Good, but I'm afraid I have to take her home right this minute or else my father is going to murder me."

You grabbed me by the hand. "Say good night to Sam."

"Good night, Sam," I said.

"Good night, Nell."

Walking back down the hill I had that vertigo feeling again, but more perilous this time, like my balance was delicate: at any moment I'd topple forward into oblivion. I wasn't drunk. I hadn't touched a drop. I didn't want to give Dad any reason to prohibit me from tagging along to the next party.

Dad has a nose on him. You know that.

I was just mad. Really, really mad. So mad at you that I couldn't even find the words to explain how I was feeling and I knew if I tried I'd start crying.

It was chilly. I hadn't brought a jacket. The moon was huge and we walked home in silence.

Maybe you thought it was a comfortable silence. Or you were just happy to not have to say anything at all, because you looked bored at the party, like talking was a major effort.

Why did you have to speak to me like that? You knew what I thought of Sam Fitzpayne. You dismissed him as a little boy, but guess what? I like boys. I liked him. You knew that. So why did you have to sound like my babysitter? Like I was a pesky child left in your care?

I have to take her home or else my father is going to murder me. Say good night to Sam.

Layla, you have a crazy power over me I can't even begin to understand. I was so hurt, so wounded, and then, after we got home and passed Dad's smell test and brushed our teeth side by side in the mirror, you reached over and put your lips to my forehead. "Good night. Love you."

Everything was forgiven.

Nothing else mattered.

IF DUNCAN AND PARKER CREED were still alive, they'd be eighteen and twenty years old.

Imagine that for a minute. I try, but I can't, just like I can't imagine them buried in the cemetery where their matching headstones overlook a little man-made "peace pond" stocked with koi, which is just a fancy name for carp.

To me they will always be fourteen and sixteen, and it's the strangest thing in the world that I'm older now than Duncan and almost as old as Parker.

There's the story we've been told. That Parker died in a freak accident. He fell down the marble stairs of their massive mansion on Broadway and hit his head in just the wrong spot. An inch or two in either direction and he'd have been okay, Dad said. I pictured a secret on/off switch just below the skull, above the neck, and I've been extra careful ever since—wearing a helmet every time I ride my bike, and I don't know if you've noticed, but I avoid headers on the soccer field.

I take these precautions even though you and I are pretty sure this version of his death is a total lie. Just like we're pretty sure that Duncan didn't drop dead of an undetected heart condition nine months later.

I have no idea if Dad knows what really happened. All I'm saying is there's something about these stories that just doesn't pass the smell test.

Yes, that staircase was a little treacherous, carved out of marble because I guess it's not enough to live in a house with an unobstructed view of the bay, you've got to have a staircase that looks like it belongs in Versailles.

Their father was Dad's college roommate at Stanford. Boatloads of money. I loved their Christmas party more than Christmas itself. It was my favorite night of the year. From the moment we'd pull up and a valet in a white jacket would take our keys and hand each of us a red rose, until we left sometime around midnight with enormous wrapped gifts, I felt like a character in a cozy picture book.

The boys wore tuxedos. That sounds pompous, but they were so adorable, and they grew up to be drop-dead gorgeous, which I know is a poor choice of words.

Santa Claus was there, and more real to me than any Santa Claus I'd ever seen, even though I didn't believe in Santa Claus because you kindly disabused me of that myth when I was only five. But in that house, I believed.

We'd see the Creeds a few other times a year. They'd

come to Dad and Sonia's, or we'd meet in a restaurant, but most often we'd go to their place, where a team of servants would cook and serve dinner at their enormous table.

Duncan and Parker were always polite and accommodating, though I'm sure there were plenty of people they'd rather have been spending time with. They'd ask if we wanted to watch a movie or play Ping-Pong in the game room.

I wouldn't have known how to tell if someone had a drug problem, but rumor has it that Parker's was cocaine. That's what you'd heard from someone who knew the Creeds at summer camp. And who knows? Maybe Parker did fall down those stairs and hit himself in the head in just the wrong place *because* he was high on drugs.

And maybe what we'd heard about Duncan, that he'd swallowed a whole bottle of pills nine months after his older brother's death because he couldn't imagine living without him, maybe that wasn't at odds with what Dad told us: Duncan died of a previously undetected heart condition.

Because that's what killed him, isn't it?

A broken heart?

IT'S TIME TO GET TO the heart of our matter. Did you change and then go looking? Or did what you find cause you to change?

Somehow I think the story begins with that self-portrait from school, the one with your faraway eyes. If I could go back to the moment I saw it, and if I had known what I was looking at, I'd have pulled you aside and said: *No. Stop. Don't.*

Remember a few years ago when that palmistry shop opened? The woman put a handwritten sign in her window:

Madam Mai can tell your future. Only 10 dollar!

Mom had given us thirty to spend on dinner. We tried talking Madam Mai into a two-for-one, but she said, "Different hands, different futures, different readings," and folded her arms.

The only palm readers I'd ever seen were in books or movies. They had flowing robes, turbans, and dangly bracelets, and they didn't look a thing like Madam Mai, who was Vietnamese, and so slight she could blow away in the breeze off the bay. She had on yoga pants, a tank top, and bare feet.

I wanted to argue that our futures were intertwined, that if she was worth her salt, she could look at your palm and tell my future or look at mine and tell yours, but I knew she wouldn't budge.

We stepped out to the sidewalk and debated. Were we ready to roll the dice with Madam Mai? We decided that if we went to the new burger joint and skipped the fries we could probably still get a decent meal, and so we went back in and forked over two ten-dollar bills.

She took us separately into a back room with red velvet walls. She must have put up that velvet to soundproof the space, because I pressed my ear to the door when it was your turn, and I couldn't hear a word.

She said I'd marry, have children, I'd find fulfillment. My lifeline was nice and long.

"You are searching," she said, staring at me meaningfully. "You have voids in your life you wish to fill. But you should know that the answers are not where you might expect to find them."

Wow.

What a total heap of steaming cow shit.

I mean, find me anyone off the street: man, woman, child. You could say everything Madam Mai said about me, and it would just as easily fit that stranger.

I came out and rolled my eyes at you. Your turn. As I mentioned, I put my ear to the door.

Nothing.

You came out minutes later with a smile stretched across your face. She held a motherly hand to your shoulder.

"Thank you so much," you said.

"My pleasure."

Out on the sidewalk you spun around like the actresses do in Dad's lame black-and-white movies.

"I'm going to fall in love," you said. "Real love. Very soon."

Okay, I'll admit it: I was jealous. Who doesn't want to fall in real love? In fact, the idea was so appealing to me that for a minute I forgot Madam Mai was a con artist who didn't even bother to dress the part.

"She's full of it," I said.

You raised one eyebrow at me. "Time will tell."

If only I could have looked at your palm and seen your future and then done something to change it.

You worked so hard on that portrait. And it was really good, despite the fact that we have no talent. Mom and Dad stocked their houses with art supplies—reams of white paper, pointy pencils, an array of colored Sharpies. We spent hours at the art table drawing, painting, cutting, gluing, never making anything worth keeping, but enjoying each other's company. Remember?

City Day takes its arts pretty seriously. What other school would stage a production of *Les Misérables*? Why not *Oklahoma!* or *Annie*? At City Day you can learn any instrument known to man, and once you learn it you can join the orchestra or the jazz ensemble or the school rock band. You can take electives in photography, graphic design, pottery, even the basics of architecture.

But every freshman must begin with Intro to Visual Arts, a survey course taught by Mr. Barr.

I made my own charcoal portrait this fall. Every freshman makes one, and I hated doing it. I hated the way the charcoal smelled, like poverty and illness, and I missed sitting at a table with you and our Sharpies. The result was a girl who looked wan and ugly.

Anyway, everyone loves Mr. Barr. He's fun and funny and he's young and he dresses cooler than any boy in school and he talks to us like we're his equals. He knows about the music we listen to. He's seen the movies we see, not the kind favored by Dad and Sonia. Going to his class feels like a break in the everyday.

You'd mentioned him to me. Lots of times. You'd never thought to mention Sam Fitzpayne, but you'd mentioned Mr. B.

I was looking forward to Intro to Visual Arts because I'd heard it was one of the best classes taught by one of the best teachers. Felix, who's genuinely talented, adored Intro to Visual Arts, and Mr. B., from day one.

That Sunday after the first week of school he'd called to ask about our Spanish homework, but I knew he was really calling to hear about the party at Hazel Porter's house, and to find out if I thought there was some sort of wormhole through the City Day space-time continuum that might allow him to make her his girlfriend.

"She's a senior, Felix," I said. "She could be your baby-sitter."

"If that's my only way in, I'll take it."

"I love you"—I really did, though I couldn't ever just come out and tell him that without turning it into a joke—"but she's so totally out of your league she's playing in a different time zone."

"Ouch."

"Sorry. Truth hurts. Want an ice pack?"

"Was she with anyone? Like, did you see her talking to anyone who's objectively better looking than I am?"

"Objectively?"

"Yes."

"No, I did not."

"Didn't think so."

I told him what I could about the party, who was talking to whom, who drank too much, who went out onto the balcony to smoke a joint, all of this reporting somewhat unreliable considering I hardly knew anyone by name.

I didn't tell him about Sam Fitzpayne. I wasn't ready to turn Sam into the official Object of My Affection.

He asked, "What do you think of Intro to Visual Arts?"

"It's fun."

"Isn't Mr. B. the coolest?"

"Yeah, he's really cool."

"Does your class have the swearing jar?"

"The huh?"

"The swearing jar. He has this jar on his desk and he says whenever someone uses a bad word in class they have to put a dollar in the swearing jar and at the end of the semester we'll have a pizza party with all the earnings. So I raised my hand and said, *Doesn't that kinda encourage swearing? Like, the more money we have the better the party is gonna be?* And he said, *Mr. De La Cruz, right?* And I said, *Felix.* And he said, *Mr. De La Cruz, you're goddamn right!* And then he took a dollar out of his wallet and put it in the jar!"

Who wouldn't love a teacher like that? Our class didn't have one, because among his many attributes, Mr. Barr is uneven and unpredictable. Sure, a swearing jar is a pretty egregious example of buying off student affection, but considering most teachers don't seem to care what you think of them, it's nice to know, I suppose, that Mr. B. actually gives a crap.

The kinds of rumors that follow Mr. Barr are textbook. Simple math.

Take one good-looking male in his mid to late twenties with a Salvador Dalí tattoo on his bicep. Add a student body that's 50 percent female and unusually mature and worldly. Put all that into a progressive environment. And *BAM:* rumors that the teacher sleeps with his students.

You told me they start up again every year before they go wherever it is rumors go to die. If they were true, you said, Mr. B. wouldn't be working at City Day anymore.

Of course I believed you; you don't lie to me. And also because it was unthinkable that any teenage girl could be lucky enough to have Mr. B. all to herself.

Your freshman year, the rumors were about Mr. B. and Yelli Rothman, who'd since gone on to study art history at Yale. Last year's star of the show was Hazel Porter, but she's a senior now, and isn't taking any art classes, so she's off the hook. In the end, everyone admits this is only gossip. But still, the rumors come back every year like the swallows at Capistrano.

This year they were slow to start. Meanwhile, you seemed less than thrilled with the everyday goings-on at school, with the talk in the halls, the parties, the boys, and even the soccer team. You seemed distant. Not like you.

I chalked it up to the stress that comes with being a junior and having to think about the future, leaving home, and knowing that your grades actually matter.

From where I was standing with my brand-new City Day student ID card, the everyday that bored you was bursting with life and electric possibility and the question of who I would become in the months that stretched out ahead.

It made me think of a fortune I'd gotten on one of our Chinatown outings with Dad. Remember? He took us to the fortune cookie factory, hidden away down a narrow little alley. Dad told us this was our secret, we should never reveal its location to anyone, or else it would lose what made it so special. I watched the old man work the machine, pressing the square of dough around the white slip of paper and into the signature crescent shape.

I opened mine as we wandered along the main drag with throngs of Chinese families doing their Sunday shopping. Such stock we put in fortune-telling. I read my words of wisdom and then crumpled up the paper and shoved it deep in my pocket because it made no sense to me and I just wanted to eat the cookie.

But I kept it, because you know me, I'm sentimental and

superstitious and also I'm a strong candidate for that reality show about hoarding. But I like to think I kept that fortune because I knew that someday it might make sense to me.

With time and patience, the mulberry leaf becomes the silk gown.

When school started this year, I was the mulberry leaf, but I was waiting. I had patience. You, Layla, were the beautiful silk gown, and I had every intention of becoming one too.

ON THE MORNING OF OUR first soccer game I woke up feeling like I had to hurl. A stomach virus? I stayed in bed, clutching my middle, and buried my face in my pillow.

It's just nerves.

I opened one eye. Parker was sitting on my desk with his feet on my chair.

Get up and put on your uniform. Grab something to eat. You'll feel better.

My stuffed animals were never this bossy.

Why are you even nervous? You know you're just gonna sit on the bench the whole time.

This is what I liked about Duncan. He never sugarcoated anything.

He sat at the foot of my bed, eying the last stuffed animal I kept in view. The rest lived high up in my closet.

I mean, no offense, he said. *But you're just a freshman.*

I checked myself. Sick or nervous?

Parker was probably right. I had game-day jitters. I needed to go downstairs and eat something. I needed to remind myself that playing soccer was one of the only things I could do well. But Duncan was probably right too; it was unlikely I'd leave the bench.

I climbed out of bed.

Atta girl, Parker said.

I rubbed my temples.

Duncan walked over to my window and peeked outside. *Fog in September,* he said, shaking his head. *What field are you playing on?*

The Polo Fields.

We used to play there.

I knew that because Dad took us to one of their games. He thought it would be good for us to see some soccer at the high school level. I doubted they remembered.

I went to my closet and took out my new City Day uniform. N. Golden. Number 13. I grabbed the purple shorts with the gray stripes down the sides. The socks, my sports bra. I laid it all out on my bed.

These are the kinds of moments that can be awkward. Duncan and Parker may not be real, but that doesn't mean I want to get naked in front of them.

I closed my eyes tight. Opened them again.

The Creeds were gone.

★ ★ ★

The crowd was larger than I'd anticipated. Maybe because it was the first game of the year. Or because the fog had lifted and it was a glorious San Francisco day, warm, blue, and sharp, and where better to spend such a day than deep in the heart of Golden Gate Park?

The most likely explanation, however, was that we were playing back-to-back with the boys' varsity, so the turnout wasn't for us.

Duncan was right. I didn't leave the bench except for huddling around Coach Jarvis as she scribbled on her white-board. I made a show of paying attention when those x's and o's and arrows had as much relevance to my life as the NASDAQ charts in Dad's *Wall Street Journal.*

We won 2–0. You played beautifully in midfield, anchoring and supporting the team. Chiara Vittorio made both goals and reaped all the glory, but neither goal would have occurred if it hadn't been for you.

Mom and Dad were there. You'd think I'd be used to seeing them together by now, since they don't let the fact that they can't live with each other, or that he's gone on to marry someone younger and, I hate to say it, more beautiful, interfere with raising us. They stood side by side and cheered together and they gave each other a high five after each of Chiara's goals.

Felix was there, of course. And a pretty decent chunk of the freshman class.

I scanned the crowd for Sam Fitzpayne while trying not to look like I was scanning the crowd. I wanted it to seem like my head was in the game on the off chance that Coach

Jarvis might soon see her way clear to making me one of those x's on her whiteboard.

No Sam. I saw your best friend, Schuyler, who didn't go to City Day but still came out to cheer you on, and I saw Liv, your City Day best friend—their rivalry put them on opposite ends of the crowd. Mr. Frank, dean of students. Ms. Palladino, head of school. I saw Mr. B.

It didn't strike me as strange that Mr. B. came out on a Saturday morning to watch a soccer game, but now, looking back, he was the only teacher there who wasn't a dean or the head of school. Attendance wasn't part of his job description. He was there because he wanted to be there.

Afterward, you said you had plans with a friend. Mom bailed because it was a Saturday and Dad takes the weekend parenting shift.

Dad asked, "How 'bout we hit up the Dumpling King and then go sit on the beach and watch the surf?"

It sounded nice. But you had your thing, Mom had hers, and Felix stood waiting for me. I felt like being with someone my own age.

"Rain check?" I asked.

"Why would we want to sit on the beach in the rain?"

Dad's sense of humor is seriously in need of an upgrade.

Felix and I walked over to the Bison Paddock. No, I do not know the difference between bison and buffalo. And I don't know why we find them so fascinating when they don't do much other than stand around and sometimes sit and occasionally graze in the grass. It's cool to have animals that look like they belong back in the Ice Age living right in the middle of San Francisco. Especially since, as Dad likes to remind us, real estate doesn't come cheap here. But if you're looking to go where the action is, you're not going to find it with the buffalo.

Felix and I like to imagine what they're thinking. We manufacture drama. Love triangles and hidden secrets and terrible betrayals.

He pointed to the one nearest to us. "He's decided that he's a woman trapped in a man's body and hasn't worked up the courage to tell his family he's about to start hormone therapy."

"She's got a spending problem." I pointed to the one sleeping under the tree. "She stays up all night buying things she doesn't need on the Home Shopping Network and then crashes hard most of the day."

Maybe what we like so much about the buffalo is the simple fact of them. They never change. They aren't going to surprise you by doing something unexpected. They're going to stand, or sleep under a tree, or graze a bit.

That's all.

Actually, the part about them never changing isn't entirely true. Buffalo have lived in Golden Gate Park since the 1890s, at least that's what the sign on the fence says, so unless they have some crazy life expectancy, they die and then get replaced by other buffalo that look just like them.

That's why we create drama for them. Lives that stay the same day in and day out don't make any sense to us.

We walked out of the park to find a café where we could get a coffee and Felix could show me some of his drawings. He clutched his sketchbook proudly to his chest.

I've never been particularly skilled at living in the moment or *being here now* or whatever it is yoga and meditation are supposed to teach you. So maybe it was the perfect weather, or the fact that we'd won 2–0, or the steadfastness of the buffalo, but at that moment I was able to appreciate how lucky I was to have a friend like Felix De La Cruz.

I'm not telling you this to impart some sort of touchy-feely wisdom about gratitude or whatever, but as I walked out of the park with Felix, I thought about how you had not one best friend, but two. Schuyler and Liv.

They were both at the soccer game.

You said you had plans with a friend, and I wondered: Liv or Schuyler?

I didn't consider the possibility that your plans were with neither of them.

REMEMBER HOW WE USED TO tell Mom everything? It's different with Dad. He's easygoing and fun to be around, but still, even with Mom's short temper and intolerance for a dropped jacket in the front hall, she's always been the one we've turned to when we needed someone to put things in perspective.

Sometimes I think about how after they broke up Mom and Dad settled in the most ironic of places: Dad on bedrock, Mom on landfill.

Dad lives in Noe Valley on solid, unmovable ground, while Mom bought a place in the Marina, which is sort of like purchasing a high-priced sand castle. The '89 earthquake practically leveled her entire neighborhood. That was before we were born, obviously, but we know the stories, and we've seen the pictures: it's only a matter of time before the next shifting of the plates mixes us up like a bunch of Boggle cubes.

So it's funny that Dad, the risk taker, and Mom, the cautious one, live in converse seismic zones.

Because Mom is our bedrock. She's the one who'll be there no matter what the tectonic plates decide. I don't want to say anything bad about Dad, because I adore him and he's a great father, but he's maybe a little bit like the castle made of sand. Fun, whimsical, not entirely reliable.

Anyway, back to telling Mom everything. I know growing up is about figuring out how to carve out private space and what to keep to yourself. That can be tricky, but I think we found it easier than most to cut Mom out because we had each other.

If I'd been in third grade instead of ninth, I'd have come home from school in those first weeks and said "Mom, there's this boy. His name is Sam. I think I kinda love him." But instead I came home and said "Fine" when she asked how it was going and "Nope" when she asked if anything interesting had happened.

You weren't more forthcoming with Mom, which wasn't anything new. But when you started to be vague with me, I wasn't about to put up with it.

Even so, it took a few weeks or so to work up the courage to ask, in a roundabout way: What gives?

I knew I couldn't just look at you meaningfully and say *What's wrong with you lately?* or *Is there something you want to tell me?*

Instead I waited until we were on the bus from Mom's to

Dad's. Usually Mom drives us or Dad picks us up, but they both had other things on their calendars, and anyway, we've always enjoyed navigating San Francisco on our own.

"Life would be so much simpler if they'd just buy me a car," you said. "It's not like they can't afford it."

"I don't think that's the point."

"What is the point, then? Some sort of lesson? What, exactly, do they think I'm learning by riding the bus?" You pointed to an advertisement above my head. "Oh, I guess it's critical I learn Dr. Laslow can brighten my smile *and* laser away my unwanted, unseemly hairs for only $999."

I looked up at Dr. Laslow and his creepy white teeth.

"Yeah, Mom and Dad can be so unreasonable," I said, even though I could see why they'd refuse to buy a barely seventeen-year-old a car. Especially in a city where no one can go more than seven miles in any direction without reaching its limits. Where did you need to get on your own? Why couldn't you just be content with riding the bus with me, or catching a lift from Mom and Dad?

Anyway, my goal wasn't to defend Mom and Dad, it was to commiserate with you, to remind you that you could talk to me.

But you were texting.

"I don't think I want to be a junior," I said.

You looked up. "What?"

"I don't ever want to be a junior."

"Why?" You went back to texting, a little annoyed.

"Because it seems too hard. Too much work and pressure and stuff."

You shrugged. "Don't worry. You're smart as shit. You'll do fine."

Strike one.

"It just sort of seems like your year is off to a bad start. Usually you're more excited about school."

"I don't know what you're talking about," you said. Translation: *Please leave me alone so I can concentrate on this text.*

Strike two.

So I decided to follow a wisp of suspicion I hardly knew I had.

"What did you do last Saturday after the game?"

You didn't look up from your phone. "Huh?"

"After the soccer game at the Polo Fields last Saturday. Where did you go?"

"The de Young."

"With Liv?" Schuyler wouldn't be caught dead at an art museum.

"No."

"Schuyler?" I asked, incredulous.

"No." You shoved your phone in your bag and looked at me. Daring and confident. "With Mr. B."

"You went to a museum with Mr. Barr? On a Saturday?"

"Shhh."

"What, is it a secret?"

"No, you're just really loud."

I was definitely using my outside voice.

"Wow."

"What?"

"That's weird, is all."

"What's weird? He's my art teacher. I'm taking a painting seminar and there was an Impressionist show at the de Young."

"Did anyone else go with you?"

"No. So?"

"So that's weird."

"You're weird."

You opened your bag, dug around for the phone you'd just put away, and went back to staring at the screen. I'd rattled you.

You could have lied to me. Told me that you'd gone to a museum or a movie or the beach with Schuyler or Liv and I'd have believed you. But you trusted me. It was a test balloon of sorts—to say out loud that you spent the afternoon alone with a teacher who has a reputation.

And I shot that balloon right out of the sky.

I'm sorry for that. I really am.

I tried telling myself maybe it wasn't so weird. City Day is a place where students are given special attention and unique opportunities to learn and grow, and blah, blah, blah.

But your neck got red. You took off your sweater. You were hot and rashy, which happens when you're caught in an uncomfortable situation, and I know because it happens to me too. When I saw the color creeping up to your face I should have backed down. I'm your sister, and I want more than anything to be on your side.

As I sat and watched you text with angry fingers, all I wanted was to get off the bus and back on your good side.

So I decided that you, like most girls at City Day, had a harmless crush on Mr. B. I decided I was reading too much into everything, as usual. I should let it go.

We were on our way to Dad's. It was a Friday night and we had no plans. I still liked these sorts of nights the best, when it was just you and me at home with some version of our family.

We hopped off at 24th and Church. I offered to carry one of your bags. You let me—accepting my olive branch.

We played Bananagrams until midnight. Sonia begged off early because she had a brief she had to work on over the weekend. You and I should have followed her, considering our game the next day was at nine against one of the strongest teams in the league. But prudence, especially while in Dad's care, is not our strong suit. Between you, Dad, and me we finished a pint and a half of Mitchell's Grasshopper Pie ice cream, after an extra-large deep-dish calamity from Paxti's Pizza.

I went to bed bloated but happy. Dad stood on the threshold to my room and said, "Good night, Monkey Number Two."

That's always been Dad's nickname for me because you are Monkey Number One.

"Good night, Pops."

"Sleep well." He kissed the top of my head.

"I'll try."

I closed the door behind him and turned around to find the Creed brothers sitting on my bed.

You ate too much, huh? Parker nodded sympathetically.

You've got a game tomorrow. You should be taking care of your body, Duncan said.

I stood and stared at them. Trying to convey with a look

46

that they were on my bed and I needed to get in it, like, immediately.

Do you want us to go?

I was so, so tired.

They stood up and I climbed under my covers, turned out the light, and closed my eyes.

Nell, Duncan whispered in the dark.

I put a pillow over my head but it didn't block the sound of his voice. *Her neck was creeping red.*

I'M SURE YOU THINK I tried out for the fall play just to get nearer to Sam Fitzpayne.

Sure, when I walked by the drama room and saw his name on the sign-up sheet it lit a fire under me and I wrote my name up there too, but it wasn't only Sam. You were changing. Pulling away from me. The survivalist in me must have known that I needed something other than soccer, other than being N. Golden, Monkey Number Two. I needed to do something for me, and yes, you'd worked on the musical your freshman year, but I wasn't following in your footsteps. I wanted to be onstage, not behind the scenes, and anyway, you know how I love me some Shakespeare.

I didn't know that Ms. Eisenstein planned on rewriting *Hamlet* to set it in present-day San Francisco.

I talked Felix into trying out too. He's got a natural flair for drama, and I told him it was a way to meet new people.

When he still looked at me skeptically, I reminded him that we'd do this together.

"Okay. Fine. But only because you're making me. Sheesh. You're such a dominatrix."

I patted him on the head. "Good boy."

"But I'm *so* not kissing you, so you'd better not try out for Ophelia."

We were sitting in the cafeteria. The only day of the week our lunch period overlapped was Wednesday, so we had a lot of catching up to do in forty-five minutes.

"For one thing, I'm not sure Hamlet ever actually gets to kiss Ophelia in the play. For another, I'm not going to try out for Ophelia because I'd never get the part and I don't like to set myself up for failure. I'm a winner, not a loser, got that Felix? And finally: you will not be Hamlet because Sam Fitzpayne will be Hamlet, because that is the way the universe works."

"Sam Fitzpayne? What's so special about Sam Fitzpayne?"

I just stared at him.

"Oh my God. You have a crush on Sam Fitzpayne."

"I do not."

"Yes you do. And why wouldn't you? He's so dreamy."

"I thought you didn't know what's so special about him."

"I was fishing. Trying to get you to admit you like him. I was just setting a trap. And you stepped right into it."

"You're mixing your metaphors."

"It's okay. Hunting and fishing go hand in hand."

We took a pause to actually eat some of our organic, locally sourced lunch. I took a look around the room.

"How come nobody sits with us?"

"Because we're boring."

"Speak for yourself."

"I mean we're boring when we're together."

"I reject that. We're not boring. At least, I'm not boring."

"Prove it."

I spied Hugh Feldman across the room. "See the guy over there in the green and blue striped sweater?"

"The preppy one?"

"Yeah. Him. I've seen his penis."

Felix put his hands over his ears. "Oh God. Please. I'm eating my lunch."

I picked up a green bean and flung it at him, then stood and collected my tray.

"Meet me in the drama room. Three-fifteen. Bring your flair."

He grinned. "I never leave home without it."

I had to go talk to Coach Jarvis because tryouts for the play conflicted with soccer practice. If I got a part, I was pretty sure I could swing both, considering whatever role I got would be minor. Soccer ended in early November. We'd put on the play in December before break. I had a speech prepared, but I didn't need to deliver it because Coach just said, "No problem."

"Really?"

"You've got to follow your passions, N. Golden. I'm not in the business of getting between kids and their passions."

"But . . ." I stopped myself from saying something as pathetic as *Don't you need me?*

"No buts. Other than yours, which you should get to the practice field pronto after knocking 'em dead at tryouts."

Kids make fun of Coach Jarvis sometimes because she's like the textbook girls' PE coach: bad tracksuit, bad haircut, tendency to bark orders faux–military style. But she's really a big softie. At least, this is what I chose to believe instead of the version whereby she didn't give a crap whether I showed up for practice or not.

I saw you in the hall that afternoon and told you about my plans. I wanted your approval, of course, but there was also a part of me that wondered if maybe you'd decide to try out too. Maybe for once *you'd* follow *me* into something.

"You'll be great, Nell. I know you will."

"I don't know . . . maybe. It just sounds like fun. And it probably won't hurt on my college applications either."

"Don't worry about that stuff yet. Just do what you want to do."

"Why don't you try out too?"

You laughed. "To be or . . . *NOT.*"

"C'mon."

"No thank you."

"Pleeeease?" How could I go out on that stage in front of an audience with lights blazing down on me and not have you nearby?

"No," you said firmly. "Acting isn't my thing. You know that. And anyway, I don't have the time."

"What is your thing, then? Art?"

I know I sounded pissy, though I wasn't sure why.

Your face fell. "Good luck today." You walked away.

Sam got the part of Hamlet and I was cast as one of Ophelia's friends. I know, I know, Ophelia doesn't have any friends in *Hamlet,* but this was Ms. Eisenstein's version. So that meant I got to be one of Ophelia's bitchy high school friends who thinks Hamlet is a big waste of her time. This truly tested my acting talents, considering we were talking about Sam Fitzpayne.

You would have made a killer Ophelia.

I just thought you should know that.

Anyway, I didn't sign up just to get closer to Sam, though that's exactly what happened. I wondered at first if he'd start dating Isabella Jones, his Ophelia, because that's how it goes with movie stars—people fall in love when they play people in love.

But I guess I was imposing a Hollywood version of falling in love onto a high school where there really isn't much use for love, or even dating. There's hookups and people who hang out and all sorts of variations, but the actual boyfriend/girlfriend is a rare breed at City Day.

There's Brian Belsen and Katie Hulquist, who've been together since they were sophomores, and if the frequency with which I've seen him shoving his tongue down her throat is any indication, I can believe they're in love. I'd heard that Hugh Feldman had started dating a freshman named Ava Price, though I couldn't confirm that, because I didn't know Hugh well enough to ask, despite the fact that I'd seen his nether regions.

Sam and I didn't get close right away. First of all, I was with Felix all the time, and I'm pretty sure Sam thought Felix and I were a couple. Everyone always thinks that. It's just part of having a boy for a best friend.

The truth is I think I did have a crush on Felix at first, but

I was in fourth grade and it was hard to sort out my feelings back then, not that it's much easier now.

All I know is that when Felix came to school as the new kid, I did everything I could to get near him. He was shorter than me by a half foot and skinny as hell.

I know this sounds cheesy, but he just crackled with life. He never stopped moving and he was always fun to be around. As he used to say: *There ain't no party like a Felix party cuz a Felix party feels good!*

Felix is still funny, and he still crackles with life, but now he doesn't feel the need to win over the room.

Felix got a great part in the play—Jess, Claudius's side-kick, who was Ms. Eisenstein's reimagining of the classic court jester, a spot-on role for him.

Since Felix and I were in about five scenes total we spent a lot of time in the back of the auditorium whispering in fake Shakespearean dialect and plotting our rise from bit players to leads in the life of the school.

Now that I'd admitted my obsession with Sam Fitzpayne, Felix had vowed to help me make some headway.

"Thou mighteth beginneth by the removal of thy peasant's head from my most regal lap," I said.

Felix was resting on me like he often does.

"'Tis all· right, milady," he said without moving. "'Tis besteth he believeth he dost have competition for thy royal heart."

What I said next I couldn't translate into our Fakespeare because it was hard enough to find the words in my native language.

I leaned in close. "The problem is," I whispered. "I think he's sort of in love with Layla."

"Pffff." Felix waved his hand in my face.

"What does that mean?"

"You think everyone's in love with Layla."

"What's your point?"

"Does Layla like him?"

"No. She thinks he's a boy."

"He is a boy."

"No, I mean she thinks he's a little boy."

"Has she seen his abs?"

"I doubt it, but now I have to ask: do *you* have a crush on Sam Fitzpayne?"

"No, I'm just jealous of his abs. How can she call him little?"

"I think we've lost our thread."

"My point is, Nell, that if Layla doesn't like Sam, then who cares if he has a thing for her. It's not gonna happen, and eventually he'll realize that and go after someone he has a chance with."

"Wow, you sure know how to make a girl feel good."

"Is that my job?"

"Sorta. Yeah."

He sat up and leaned back against the wall next to me. He draped his leg over mine and nudged my foot.

"You're every bit as awesome as Layla. It just takes someone with some vision to recognize that."

"Honestly, Felix? You suck at this."

"Would it help if I said I think Sam is looking at you?"

I shielded my eyes from the stage. "You're lying. You're just trying to slap a Band-Aid on a wound."

I glanced up through my fingers at Sam, who was holding Ophelia's hands and staring directly into her eyes.

"Patience, Nell," Felix said. "We're just getting started. By the time we're done with the play, we'll all know each other inside and out. That's what happens with things like school plays. And, well . . . to know you is to love you. That's all I'm trying to say."

"So . . . the play's the thing?"

He nodded. "The play's the thing."

"Oh, my liege." I rested my head on his shoulder and took his hand in mine. "You are most gentle and most kind."

IN MIDOCTOBER YOU STARTED LAYING the ground-work for ditching our annual girls' weekend with Mom and Gramma. First you blamed it on soccer. We had a game that Saturday, like we always do, but you'd never minded missing one before, so that argument didn't hold up.

Then you said you had too much homework.

I know when you're trying to get out of something you don't want to do. But it made no sense that you'd want to miss our trip to Big Sur—we loved that trip—and so against my better judgment I accepted your homework excuse.

There are so many reasons to love our weekend with Mom and Gramma. For one thing, it's a ritual, and in a life as fractured as ours, I treasure something that's a constant year in, year out. I assumed you did too. For another thing, that hotel kicks ass. The sheets. The bathrobes. The breakfast spread. I could go on.

When we first began our annual girls' trip, we went camping. That was when you and I were younger, and Gramma was younger, and the allure of pitching a tent beneath the towering redwoods was stronger than the hands of Manny, who gives us our massages at the resort we traded up for a few years back. I'm all about nature, breathing in the scent of pine and listening to the crashing surf, but I prefer to do so from the deck of our two-bedroom suite.

You're even more of a spa whore than me. You took to the idea of someone rubbing orange-scented exfoliant onto your face and coconut oil on your naked body way more quickly than I did. That first year we went to the resort, I stayed in the room and watched pay-per-view while you and Mom and Gramma got pampered, but whatever hang-ups I had have vanished. Nowadays I say: bring on the treatments.

I asked, "Why can't you just bring your homework?"

"I don't want it to ruin the vibe."

Let me give you two reasons this weekend should never be jettisoned for anything as mundane as homework:

We spend weekends with Dad, but this is the one time Mom gives over her Saturday and Sunday entirely to us. You say Mom is selfish, that she's more concerned with landing a husband than hanging out with her daughters, but you can be too hard on her. So *this* is our weekend with Mom. Don't call her selfish or complain she's too busy and then make up some lame-ass excuse for why you can't come.

I hate to beat a dead horse, but this is a *ritual,* okay?

That means it takes precedence over everything. And you know why we do it. We go every year on the anniversary of Gramma's mother's death. And even though we never knew her, it's like this time when we're supposed to feel the thread connecting the women of our family across the generations or something, and maybe that's bullshit, but who cares? It's important.

I was surprised when Mom caved. She said she understood the pressure you were under and how seriously you took your schoolwork. She said she admired your drive. And then when Dad said that he and Sonia were going to be away that weekend on a trip they'd planned ages ago because he knew we'd all be in Big Sur, Mom said, "Okay. You're mature enough to stay home on your own."

You could have scraped my jaw off Mom's kitchen floor.

It's like our dream. All we've ever wanted, really, is a weekend to ourselves in one of our parents' houses. We've planned it all out. Mapped an itinerary. At Mom's we'd leave dishes in the sink and our clothes and shoes all over the house and nobody would yell at us to pick up after ourselves. At Dad's there's not much we'd do that he doesn't let us do already, except maybe have a raging party with nobody around to smell the alcohol on us afterward.

I asked you flat out: "Are you having a party?"

"Are you insane? Just imagine one of Mom's precious knickknacks getting bumped a few degrees in the wrong direction. She'd have my ass on a plate."

"Layla," I said. Giving you my best *I'm your sister, you can't lie to me* look.

"I'm not, Nell, okay? Haven't you noticed that I don't like parties all that much? I just have heaps of work to do and the team is undefeated, and not to sound conceited or anything, but I take some responsibility for that, so I shouldn't miss the game, and also, it'll be really nice to just spend a weekend alone."

Okay, so that stung a little.

Okay, maybe it stung a lot.

We packed up Mom's car Friday afternoon. We didn't need much; weekend attire is mostly the hotel bathrobe. You stood in the doorway in your bare feet and I wondered if you were thinking: *To hell with the team, to hell with homework.*

Mom gave you the neighbors' contact information in case of emergency and went over her list of rules. Lock the doors. Set the alarm. Make sure you turn the stove burners all the way off so you don't fill the house with gas.

It's funny where our parents think the dangers lurk.

As we pulled out of the driveway Mom rolled down her window and called, "Oh, and, Layla, honey?"

"Yeah?"

"No friends over, okay? I wouldn't feel right about that. Parents expect there to be a chaperone."

You held up the book in your hand. "Homework, Mom. Remember?"

She blew you a kiss.

You blew one back.

I rarely got to sit in the front seat—you'd claimed it as your birthright—and my reign was brief, only until we arrived at the airport to collect Gramma flying in from

Chicago. When we pulled onto the 101, I turned to look back at the city. I loved this view. I loved it coming and I loved it going. It filled me with a sense of belonging—*this is my home.* But on this day the view filled me with *longing,* without the *be.* Longing for you. You were only twelve minutes in my rearview mirror and I was already missing you. I realize now that the longing and the missing started before that drive.

I must have sighed or something. Or maybe it showed on my face.

"You okay, kiddo?" Mom asked.

"Yeah, I'm fine."

She reached over and took my hand. It felt nice, but I was too old to hold Mom's hand. I counted to three and then pulled away, pretending I needed to check my phone.

She let her forsaken hand rest on my knee. "How're things?"

Mom was smarter than this, but maybe she'd had a long week. She knew these sorts of open-ended inquiries never got her anywhere.

"Fine."

"Are you enjoying City Day?"

"Yes."

"New friends?"

"Uh-huh." This was pretty much a lie, but I didn't feel like going into detail about how I mostly hung out with Felix, or girls from the soccer team who were more your friends than mine.

"Okay . . . who has the worst BO in the whole school?"

This was more like Mom. "Hands down, Coach Nolan."

"Coach Nolan? I thought you had Coach Jarvis."

"Coach Jarvis is the soccer coach. Coach Nolan teaches freshman PE."

"And she stinks?"

"Totally. You'd think if you're gonna choose a life in physical education, you might work out the deodorant thing first."

"So, who's the dumbest kid in school?"

"I don't know . . . everyone seems pretty smart."

"That's not fair! Now you're just making me look catty while you look magnanimous."

"If the shoe fits."

She laughed. "Who's the cutest boy? And don't say Felix. You know I love Felix and I think he's adorable, but he doesn't count."

I made a show of thinking it over.

"I guess Sam Fitzpayne."

"Sam Fitzpayne . . . I like the sound of that. Sam Fitz- payne . . . he could be a hard-boiled private eye. Or an MP in the House of Commons. Or maybe a late-night newscaster: 'This is Sam Fitzpayne, signing off.'"

She'd lost me. I was staring out the window into the white lights of the oncoming traffic and thinking about Sam and his one-dimpled smile.

"Hey, kiddo," she said.

"Yeah?"

"I'm sorry Layla didn't come along too. I really am."

"Yeah."

"It was bound to happen. I guess we should consider ourselves lucky it lasted as long as it did."

"What are you talking about?"

We were driving on the big, arced bridge that led to the arrivals terminal. It always felt to me a little like coming in for a landing.

"I mean it was only a matter of time before her private life became more important to her than what she does with her family. That's part of growing up. It'll happen to you too, it probably already is happening to you. And that's okay. It really is, even though I'd much prefer for you to always be my baby."

"She had homework, Mom. It's not like she didn't want to be with us."

"Right," Mom said distractedly. She'd spied Gramma standing out on the curb with a knit wool hat and her roller bag. She opened her window and waved excitedly. Gramma waved back.

"It's okay," Mom said as she pulled up to the curb. "Because someday you and your sister will do exactly this. You'll come to an airport somewhere to pick me up and all you'll want to do is be with me, with someone who knows and understands you, and we'll spend the whole weekend talking."

She jumped out and threw her arms around Gramma. They held on to each other. I felt I was watching a private moment. One in which I had no place.

"Nellie!" Gramma shouted. I ran to her and let her pull me into their embrace.

She took a look around. "Where's Layla?"

I couldn't believe Mom hadn't warned her you were bailing. In that moment I saw that Mom is still Gramma's kid, afraid of disappointing her or failing to meet her expectations.

"Well . . . she had a tremendous amount of homework and this is her junior year, so her grades are critical, and you know Layla, she's so responsible, she just didn't feel she could take the time."

"Poppycock," Gramma said.

"Mother," Mom said as she hoisted Gramma's bag into the trunk. "If you don't want to seem ancient, you really shouldn't say *poppycock.*"

This is why Mom didn't tell Gramma in advance. Because Gramma knows things. She knows the truth from poppycock.

We managed to have a good time without you. I guess it's hard not to enjoy yourself when your every need is catered to so extravagantly. Mom allowed me a glass of champagne at dinner and I didn't like the way it tasted, but I drank it anyway.

We texted a few times. You described your weekend alone as *busy* and *boring.* Those seemed like contradictory descriptions, but I didn't point that out.

Saturday after dinner and the champagne, I came back to my room, the one we were supposed to share. I imagined Parker and Duncan sprawled out on what should have been your bed, wearing white bathrobes.

Man, this place is nice, Duncan said.

Parker nodded. *Yeah, you can just feel your worries melting away.*

I went into the bathroom to change into my pajamas, and when I came back out Parker asked, *Where's your robe?*

I didn't need my robe. I was wearing pajamas.

C'mon, Duncan prodded. *Get your robe on. That's the tradition. You're supposed to hang out in your robe.*

I grabbed it from the hook on the door and threw it on. I climbed into my bed.

Now what do we do? Parker asked. *What would you be doing if Layla had come?*

If you'd come, Layla, we'd sit around and talk. Or watch a movie. And we'd eat the chocolates from our pillows.

I picked up the gold, foil-wrapped chocolate from your bed.

See, now you get to eat both. That's a bonus, right?

I swallowed it whole, barely tasting it.

We know you miss her. We know it's more fun when you're together.

But you were busy. You had "heaps of homework."

That's what she said. Do you believe her?

I wanted to believe you.

But do you?

Did I?

Parker pointed to the remote control on the stand between us. *C'mon. Let's watch a movie.*

I picked it up and switched on the flat-screen TV.

Let's watch something fun. Something to take your mind off things. How about a romantic comedy?

I thought guys hated romantic comedies. I thought they only liked science fiction or sports or something where lots of stuff gets blown up.

Maybe most guys, but not us.

They leaned back against their headboard, facing the screen. I was glad to not be alone, but something about the two of them in their matching robes in bed next to each other made me feel even lonelier than had I not conjured them at all.

Choose something that'll make us laugh, Duncan said. *Something with a happy ending.*

THE RUMORS STARTED ON MONDAY.

So-and-so told so-and-so that someone had seen you downtown on Saturday night with Mr. Barr. One report had you coming out of the W Hotel. The other had you walking up 3rd Street with his arm around your waist.

I heard it first from Felix, who slipped me a note in Spanish class.

Es verdadero?

Is it true? I didn't know how to write *Is WHAT true?* So instead I just wrote:

Que?

What?

I slipped it back to him. He scribbled something and slid it over.

Su hermana y Señor Barr?

I looked at him across the desk of the girl who sat between us, and he flashed me a signature Felix devilish grin, which disappeared when he saw my shocked face.

He shrugged at me. A sort of body apology.

I so rarely got mad at Felix that I didn't know how to handle it when I did. My strategy that day was to make a beeline for the door as soon as we were dismissed, but Felix caught up in the hallway.

"Hey." He grabbed my wrist.

"What?"

"Why are your panties all in a knot?"

"Why are you spreading rumors about Layla?"

"How does writing a note to you classify as spreading rumors?"

"What have you heard?"

"Nell, calm down."

"Don't tell me to calm down. And you know how I hate the word *panties*."

"Sorry. Geez."

"What have you heard?"

Felix looked around. He lowered his voice. "Nothing. I mean, not nothing, but I just heard that there's something up with Layla and Mr. B. You know there's always a rumor about Mr. B. and somebody. They're never true. Anyway, I just thought you'd think it was funny that it's Layla. But I was wrong. And stupid. I'm sorry."

He reached into his backpack, took out his sketch pad, and ripped out a page.

"Here." He handed it to me.

A perfect drawing of a buffalo. "Why are you giving me this?"

"Penance."

"Huh?"

"To show you that I'm truly sorry."

It was hard to get mad at Felix, and even harder to stay mad.

"Thanks. I'll treasure this."

"Let's blow off our next classes and go hang out and talk."

"I can't, Felix."

"Why not?"

"Because I can't cut classes. That's not what I do."

"Okay. How about blowing off play rehearsal? We have no scenes today."

"That I think I can swing."

We met out on the steps after school and walked over to the coffee shop we liked. Felix was obsessed with their cherry pie. As you know, I've never been a fan of pie, so I ordered a mocha latte.

I looked for you that afternoon but couldn't find you. I worried about you, because I had no idea what the hell was going on. I wanted to hear from you that you were okay. That you weren't freaking out.

I called you on our walk over to the coffee shop. You didn't pick up, so I sent a text:

U OK?

I put my phone on the table between Felix and me. Willed it to vibrate with your answer.

I folded my arms and glared at him. "So tell me everything you know."

"I don't know anything. I just heard that someone saw them together. On like Saturday night. Or something." Felix put his hands up in mock defense. "But obviously Layla wasn't with Mr. B. on Saturday night, right?"

"I don't think so."

"What do you mean you don't *think* so?"

"I mean I think she was home alone this weekend catching up on homework and stuff. And anyway, even if they were together, it doesn't mean something is happening between them."

"It doesn't? Really? Do you know what I was doing Saturday night?"

"No."

"I was at a baseball game with my dad. Do you know what I was *not* doing on Saturday night?"

"No."

"I was *not* out with Ms. D'Amato, sharing a plate of spaghetti, each of us with a strand in our mouths like those freaking dogs from that Disney cartoon. And do you know why?"

"Because she has a huge butt?"

"That, and because it would be inappropriate."

"Okay, just to play devil's advocate . . . what if there was, like, an exhibit at the Academy of Sciences about chemistry and she asked you if you wanted to go see it because you're her star chemistry student?"

"First of all, I'm terrible at chemistry. Second of all, it would be weird if she just asked me to go and not the rest of my class. And third of all, why does the devil always need an advocate? Don't you think he can argue things for himself?"

Weird. That's the word I'd used too. *Weird* that you were the only student who went with Mr. Barr to the Impressionist show at the de Young.

My phone buzzed.

Fine. ☺

I know texting is limited in what you're able to communicate, but I found this response baffling. Did you not know people were talking? Did you know and not care? Had you managed to shut it down by offering an alibi? And why on earth were you smiling?

I showed Felix my phone.

"See?" he said. "Everything is fine. She's smiling. Crisis averted."

I took a sip of my latte, now cold. "So tell me about your weekend. How was the baseball game?"

"We left after the sixth inning."

"A blowout?"

"No, my dad got tired. He gets tired a lot. I, on the other hand, have boundless energy. I stayed up until three in the morning. Look." He pulled his sketchbook out and opened it up to a beautiful, intricate ink drawing of a girl. Hazel Porter. "What do you think?"

"Another buffalo?"

"Bite your tongue!"

"It's awesome, Felix."

"What'll she think?"

"That you're a major talent. And a total creeper."

He laughed. "Chicks dig this shit. Remember Bethany?"

"You went out with her for like five minutes in eighth grade."

"Yes, but I believe she still has the drawing I did of her hanging in her room. This is why there are always rumors about Mr. B.: we artists have a way with the ladies."

I got home before you. On days we don't have soccer practice you sometimes stay and work in the library or go out with friends, and nobody asks about it unless you're a no-show at the dinner hour, which at Mom's is seven o'clock.

When I came home at five-thirty, the house was empty and Mom had left some twenties and a note: *Order dinner. Choose wisely. I'll be home by 7 to eat my fair share.*

I flipped through our folder of takeout menus. I was sick of every one of the restaurants, so I went through the pantry and the fridge and I managed to put together a halfway decent lentil stew. I poached an egg for the top because I believe an egg on top of anything makes it better.

You beat Mom home by only a few minutes.

"OhmygodLaylawhatsgoingon?"

You hadn't even put down your book bag.

"Whoa," you said. "Chill."

"Seriously, Layla. What the frack?"

"Are you talking about how Mr. B. and I rented the presidential suite at the W Hotel and went at it all weekend long like a couple of rabbits?"

"Something like that."

"Everyone at school must be seriously bored."

"How can you stay so calm?"

"Because I don't give a crap."

People usually say they don't give a crap when they mean

the opposite. I looked for your signs—a flushed neck, a clenched jaw, an inability to sit still. Nothing. You really didn't care.

You grabbed the lemonade, took a big swig right out of the carton, and watched as I put the finishing touches on my stew.

"So you weren't downtown with Mr. Barr?"

I practiced this three times in my head before I said it, trying to rid it of any trace of judgment.

You sighed. "No, Nell. I wasn't downtown *with* Mr. Barr."

I tried to ignore your tone and let the relief wash over me. But . . . there was something about the way you'd said *with*.

I wanted to, I really, really wanted to, but I just couldn't let it go.

"So you weren't downtown?"

"No, actually, I *was* downtown."

"Was Mr. Barr downtown?"

"Yes, he was. And I ran into him. I'd gone to SFMOMA to look at the Rothko for my essay that was due today. He was at SFMOMA too, no great surprise considering he's an art teacher. We ran into each other. Chatted on the sidewalk. Big deal. Why are you interrogating me? Maybe you should join Sonia's law firm."

"I'm just trying to figure out how the rumor started."

"Who cares?"

"I do. Why don't you?"

"Guess what, Nell? This has absolutely nothing to do with you, so why don't you just back off."

The floor beneath us rumbled with the sound of Mom opening the automatic garage door.

You looked at me. Pleading. "Will you please shut up about this around Mom? We do not need to make this the topic of tonight's dinner conversation."

"God, Layla. I wouldn't say anything to Mom."

Of course I wouldn't say anything to Mom. You know how I hate when things get tense with the two of you. Like when she wouldn't let you go to that boy/girl sleepover party in Sonoma at the end of eighth grade and you muttered *bitch* under your breath, and she totally freaked and I swore to her that she was hearing things. I try to ease friction. That's my job.

"Okay, then don't."

Over dinner Mom asked you to tell her more about your weekend and you told her it was relaxing and a little too quiet. You never once made eye contact with me. We talked about Mom's new project at work, how the play was coming along, the soccer team.

I knocked on your door after helping Mom with the dishes, but you were at your desk with your headphones on, and you waved me away.

I went to my room and called Felix and told him that you ran into Mr. B. and that was it. A chance meeting on the street.

"So can you, like, set the record straight?"

"I'll do my best," he said, "but I don't know why anyone would bother listening to me."

"Because you're persuasive. You're smarter than the devil. You don't need an advocate."

"Well, when you put it that way."

"And, Felix?"

"Yeah?"

"Don't give that picture to Hazel Porter. It's too much."

"Don't worry. I wasn't going to show it to anybody but you."

Sam Fitzpayne noticed that I'd missed play practice.

Till that point I hadn't even been sure Sam knew my first name.

"Hey, Nell," he said when I walked into Friday's rehearsal. "Where you been?"

"Yeah," I said. "Sorry. Some stuff came up."

He stepped closer. "Everything okay with you?"

I could have died right then and there. The way he looked at me, I almost wished I'd had some grave illness or tragedy, anything to draw him nearer, to bring out more of that . . . what was it? Sam-ness? It was empathy, I guess, and if empathy means feeling what it's like to be in someone else's shoes, then I wondered if Sam could feel how fast my heart was beating.

"Yeah, I'm okay. It's just been a crappy week."

"Come here," he said, and he led me over to an aisle seat in the auditorium. He sat in the seat behind me. This I didn't understand until I felt his hands on my shoulders. He started to squeeze.

He leaned forward and whispered in my ear, "How does that feel?"

How did he think it felt? As Shakespeare might put it: *so hallowed and so gracious . . . and so totally awesome.*

"Nice." I closed my eyes. He dug his thumbs into the space between my shoulder blades and then marched them up the back of my neck to the base of my scalp.

"Hamlet! Ophelia!" Ms. Eisenstein bellowed. "Front and center."

"Gotta go." He jumped up and ran to the stage. Felix slid into the seat next to me.

"Holy shiteth!" he mumbled. "Thou hast been fondled most foully by his cunning mitts."

"Shut up," I said. "You're kinda ruining the moment."

I sat still, trying to make my skin remember Sam's fingers.

"I'd give you a high five or something," Felix whispered, "but that might look a bit obvious."

"Ya think?"

"Nell. Take it from a guy. We don't touch girls like that unless we want to touch them in other places too."

I swatted him on the leg. "Don't be gross."

"Desire isn't gross, my friend, it's beautiful."

"What greeting card did you get that from?"

He laughed and gave me a congratulatory punch on the arm. We sat and watched Ms. Eisenstein directing Sam and Isabella. I thought about Sam touching me in other places. It thrilled and terrified me.

You know that I haven't had a ton of experience with fooling around or sex. I'm okay with that, I really am, because I feel like it's been my choice. I know you've had more experience, and boyfriends, and I probably could have had more experience too if I'd wanted, but I'd chosen to, you know, keep it pretty clean for the most part. Maybe if I hadn't had Felix around I'd have had a boyfriend in middle school. Other girls did, but from what I could tell it just meant they texted all the time and wrote each other declarations of love on Facebook and sometimes fooled around and then whispered about it later like they were embarrassed. I was pretty sure I got more out of my friendship with Felix than they got out of those boys they'd roped into their romantic plotlines.

Since there's no point in not being totally honest with you, I have to tell you something. Remember when I went to that party last summer with Hannah, that girl from camp? I see her sometimes, mostly in the summer, and I'm happy to hang out with her, but when long stretches of time go by when I don't see her, it's fine in a way it would never be with Felix. Anyway, I went to spend the night at Hannah's and we went to a party with her older sister, who is nothing like you. She's mean and she barely tolerates Hannah, although she did let us tag along with her, which I guess was pretty cool.

I met a guy there who was in town visiting his cousin. He'd tagged along to the party too. Anyway, before I knew it, we were out on an upstairs porch, in side-by-side reclining chairs, totally making out. His name was Kevin. He was cute and he smelled nice and we kissed for what seemed like forever.

You're probably wondering why I'm telling you all this when I already told you on the Sunday morning I came back from Hannah's. Why am I telling you something you already know?

Because here's what really happened. Here's what I didn't tell you:

Kevin and I squeezed onto one of those two reclining chairs and we kissed and our hands wandered and snaps and buttons and zippers were undone all over the place and we didn't keep it clean, far from it, and I guess I was sort of embarrassed by the whole thing. I'm not totally sure why. Maybe because we didn't even say good-bye to each other that night. Maybe because I had absolutely no idea what I was doing and I left with the feeling that I'd let him down. That there were things I should have done that I didn't. Or that I should have done what I did do better.

I just felt so confused and, honestly, a little sickened by the whole thing. That evening when I'd gotten ready in Hannah's bedroom I had no idea that by the end of the night I'd be readjusting most of my clothing, packaging myself up again to look like my life hadn't taken this unexpected detour.

I told Hannah, who'd spent most of the party looking for me, exactly what I told you. I told her that we kissed and that it was nice, that he was sweet, because that was the version of events I wanted to believe, that I wanted to remember, and it's funny because it pretty much worked out that way until right about now.

Listen: we didn't have actual sex. I was nowhere near ready for that, certainly not with someone's random cousin, and he didn't try or anything, but still, lines were crossed, and anyway, if I had had sex, I totally would have told you even if I'd been super embarrassed, because I could never imagine something so major happening in my life without telling you about it.

Can you say the same thing? Can you imagine something major in your life, a rite of passage, a game changer—can you imagine something happening that's bigger than big and *not* telling me about it?

Can you?

I think you can.

Actually, Layla, I know you can.

LET IT BE KNOWN TO the world that a small miracle occurred on Saturday, the twelfth of November.

I, N. Golden, professional benchwarmer and freshman mascot, played in eight whole minutes of our semifinal game against Brick-Moreland.

When Coach Jarvis shouted at me to take the field, I sat there, stunned, convinced she was mistaking me for you. Even though she told me to go in and replace you, I thought there must be some mistake.

"Move it, N. Golden. Now."

I jumped up and pulled off my sweats and my beanie. It was freezing and the fog was thick as cotton and my legs felt slow and stiff and I shouted, "Layla!" across the field and you looked up and saw me running toward you, and you could have been angry—this was the semifinals—but you grinned and you ran toward me and you gave me a squeeze and said, "Make me proud," and you took my seat on the bench.

I didn't embarrass myself out there, but I didn't have one of those made-for-TV moments either. I didn't score a goal or make a save or manage a theatrical header. I just did my best and got in a few decent passes and one throw-in to Alice Morrow that landed in the sweet spot.

Brick-Moreland played well, but we played better, and we made it into the finals.

We were hosting the post-game pizza party again at Dad's. I'd had such a good time the year before, imagining myself as one of the players, and I could hardly believe that here I was now, an actual Lightning team member heading into the *actual* finals.

It isn't all that often that moments serve as real reminders of the passing of time, but this was one of them. Last year I wasn't on the team, I didn't go to City Day, and there was still some nagging concern that maybe I wouldn't even get into the school, let alone make varsity, but here I was twelve short months later, and everything that seemed so out of reach back then was now part of my everyday life.

Felix begged for an invitation.

"It's strictly Lightning-only," I said.

"What about avid fans? I haven't missed a single game. And by the way, you were seriously awesome out there."

"Thanks, Felix, but you can't flatter your way into the party."

The crowd was still milling around. Teams from other schools had shown up for the next game. Golden Gate Park was awash in purple and gold and green and red and blue and white. A rainbow of jerseys cutting through the thick gray mist.

I lost you. I stood with Felix, Dad, Mom, and Sonia.

I searched the throngs of people, eying the stands, an anxiety welling in me like you were a toddler lost in an amusement park. I'd had enough bench time before Coach Jarvis threw me in to take an inventory of the crowd. Mr. Barr was there, though he wasn't the only teacher. The closer we got to the finals, the more the whole community started to come out to support us, but still, I worried you were standing somewhere with him, in plain sight. The rumors had started to settle down, and I didn't want any new fuel for the fire.

"Who's a soccer star?" you shouted as you ran toward us and threw your arms around me, messing my hair like I was a dog.

"Me?" Felix asked. You humored him by pulling him into our embrace. I was so thoroughly happy in that moment that I felt my eyes sting with tears.

"How about some celebratory dumplings?" Dad and his dumplings. He's such a one-trick pony.

Mom said she'd love to but she was running late for something or other. It's great that Mom and Dad and Sonia can share the stands at a soccer game, but sitting around a table with a lazy Susan is something else entirely. We were all relieved.

"Sounds delish," Felix said.

"Well, join us, then," Dad said.

We turned and started walking toward the parking lot, but you didn't budge.

"Listen, guys, dumplings sound great, really great, but I have plans to go hang out. I'll meet you back at the house this afternoon. Before the party. Promise."

"Layla," I said.

"What?"

"Come with us."

"No can do."

"Layla."

"What?"

I just stared at you. I gave you my best *don't do this* look.

"Nell. I'm going to go hang out with some friends. Stop trying to control me."

"Now, girls," Dad said. "Let's not bicker." He sounded like a dad on a sitcom. We hardly ever fought, and I detected a sort of satisfaction coming off Dad, as if he were enjoying doing the job we'd robbed him of all these years.

"Fine," I said, and started waking quickly toward the car. Felix jogged to catch up with me.

"What was that about?"

"Nothing."

"Nothing?"

"I don't know. I'm just worried about her."

"You're worried about Layla? The awesomely perfect Layla?"

"Just all the gossip and stuff."

"That? Who cares? Nobody really believes that. They just say it because they figure if anyone could have Layla it would have to be the hot art teacher. Some people—you, primarily—are unduly infatuated with her."

"You are too, you know."

"*Moi?* No offense, but she's not all that."

Something about this was nice to hear, that Felix didn't worship you. He didn't harbor a secret crush. But it wasn't what I needed at this moment. What I needed to hear was that you were telling me the truth. That you actually were meeting friends your own age and I had no reason to worry or wonder. But of course Felix couldn't tell me that.

"Did you see Sam?" he asked.

"What?"

"Sam Fitzpayne. Did you see him?"

"He wasn't there."

"Yes, he was. He showed up after halftime."

I'd searched the stands top to bottom, but not in the second half. I felt my heart lift.

Felix knocked into me with his shoulder. "I assumed you'd paid Coach Jarvis to put you in just so he wouldn't know you never play."

"Nope. She arrived at that insane decision on her own."

"Well, you nailed it out there," Felix said. "You always do."

I took his hand and gave it a squeeze. I can do that. I can hold on to Felix's hand in public and it isn't awkward or anything, it just makes me feel connected and important and essential to him.

The dumplings were good. The dumplings are always good. I'll never understand how they manage to put the soup on the inside.

As you promised, you showed up at Dad's in the afternoon. I'd had a nice lunch out with Dad and Sonia and Felix, and I'd played eight whole minutes, and we were headed to the finals, and I was still buzzing with the knowledge that Sam had showed up at the game, and I didn't want to ruin anything by giving you some sort of third degree, so I just said, "Hey," when you walked in.

Dad sent us to the store for paper plates and cups and napkins and stuff. We actually found ones with soccer balls on them, which just seemed too corny not to buy. We went home and painted signs and put up purple streamers. There we were, both high school students, the days of birthday parties and clowns and balloons far in our past, yet it kind of felt like being a kid again.

By the time the first guest arrived, I was giddy with excitement.

It's astonishing how much pizza fifteen girls can put away. We left a graveyard of crusts. We made ice cream sundaes in the kitchen and I took the whipped-cream and sprayed it in Chiara Vittorio's face. She asked politely if she might borrow the can. Then she returned the favor. It got a little out of hand as whipped-cream mustaches and nipples started springing up. We laughed like a bunch of drunken frat boys.

It goes without saying that we never would have gotten away with this sort of behavior at Mom's house.

We settled in the living room for the obligatory viewing of *Bend It Like Beckham*. I stretched out on the floor with some pillows. It wasn't until the scene of the pickup game in the park, where Jules spots Jess playing with the boys and kicking their asses, that I noticed you were gone. It's our favorite scene. I looked up to make eye contact with you, but your seat was empty.

I stood up.

"Grab me another soda, will you, N. Golden?" Chiara asked.

"Sure."

I didn't go into the kitchen. I went down the hallway to your closed door.

I thought about knocking. I did. But since you were shutting me out—I had no choice but to barge in.

Anyway, who disappears from her own party?

You were sitting at your desk, facing the wall, and I was able to catch a glimpse of your laptop. You snapped it shut, but I saw the screen.

"What the hell?" you shouted, and swiveled around in your chair, your face a mash-up of surprise and anger.

"I was wondering where you'd gone."

"That doesn't explain why you didn't knock."

I didn't tell you that my failure to knock was calculated precisely so I might catch you doing something you didn't want me to see.

Like video chatting.

With Mr. Barr.

While you glared at me, I felt something shifting. A fault line forming. I stood on one side, and you stood on the other.

I'll probably always remember where I was and what I wore and all that; it was that kind of moment.

I could no longer pretend.

Something *was* happening.

Something that shouldn't be.

I managed to say, "Come back and watch the movie."

Your face softened and you smiled. Relief. You thought I hadn't seen. That I was clueless. The little sister, N. Golden, Monkey Number Two.

"Go ahead," you said. "I'll catch up with you in a minute, *soccer star.*"

Earlier that day that moniker almost brought me to tears. Now I heard the condescension.

You were playing me for a fool.

"I'll save your seat." I backed out of the room.

You came out about five minutes later. This movie that I loved so much played out slowly and torturously. I didn't even crack a smile at the end when they all sing and dance to that "Hot Hot Hot" song.

Chiara slept over and everyone else left. This wasn't the plan, but you begged her, you offered her spare pajamas and a toothbrush from the collection of fresh ones Sonia keeps in the linen closet.

Chiara wasn't one of your besties, and she'd certainly never spent the night, but I guess you were desperate to have someone act as a buffer between us. I couldn't exactly barge in and ask why you were video chatting with Mr. B. while Chiara stretched out on your floor in your old Giants T-shirt and flannel bottoms.

I went to bed and I tossed and turned for hours, trying to ignore the Creed brothers.

Nell. You up?

Nell. You saw what you saw.

Nell. Nell? There's no arguing with what you saw.

Nell. Hey, Nell.

I squeezed my eyes shut tight. You had no problem leaving me alone. Why couldn't they?

Sleep changed things a bit. I still knew what I knew and I knew it for sure, but the night had erased some of the urgency. I wanted to be thoughtful. Careful. I didn't want to come off as the outraged and bewildered younger sister, I wanted to come to you like a friend with no stake in what was happening.

But you had no stake in any of it—I know that's what you're thinking. Now I'd like to try and tell you why this isn't so. Here goes:

Our lives are intertwined.

I don't know how to make this any clearer. From my surprise birth to my mistaken name, *Nellayla,* to all the nights we slept in the same room to all the days we've been each other's only constant—it could be Mom's day or Dad's, but we were almost always together—to my arrival at City Day, where I joined your soccer team, I could go on and on.

Our lives are intertwined.

This is another way of saying that I love you, Layla. I love you, and what you do matters to me, but more than that, it matters *for* me.

Think of the Creeds. I know they meant more to me than they meant to you, and I'm sure you think my fascination with them is strange or morbid, but one thing we know is that Duncan couldn't live without Parker. If such unspeakable tragedy can have a lesson, then that's what their lives and deaths taught us. Duncan had a stake in Parker's choices.

I'm obviously not talking about killing myself. I'm not trying to be overly dramatic. I'm just saying that we're close like that. We are the Goldens. And who knows; maybe to someone else out there, we are the perfect, beautiful sisters who have it all. Wouldn't that be nice? To be seen that way? But of course, another thing the Creeds have taught us is that things are more complicated when you take a closer look.

We are the Goldens, but we aren't perfect. We're going to have some hard times, and I wanted to calmly and wisely say some version of this to you: *I am your sister, I'm here to help, we're close, our lives are intertwined, you can trust me.*

Unfortunately, that didn't happen.

Chiara left around noon and you said you were going back to sleep because the two of you had stayed up all night talking.

Talking about what? Did you tell her? Did she know? How could you tell Chiara something you hid from me?

I followed you into your room.

"Nell, I need a nap. I'm seriously wiped."

"I know. I just wanted to talk."

"You always want to talk." You did a little motion with your hand. *Blah, blah, blah.* "Can't it wait a few hours?"

The calm I'd been cultivating all morning was seeping out of me.

"I saw you," I said.

"You saw me what?"

"I saw you on your computer. Last night. When I came to find you during the movie. I saw what you were doing."

"What was I doing, Nell? Enlighten me."

"Video chatting with Mr. Barr."

"And?"

"And that's what I saw."

"So?"

"So, he's a teacher. You're a student."

You smiled at me. I'd rather you'd called me a name or told me to get the hell out of your room. There was something so aggravating about that smile.

"Like I said, I'm super tired."

"Why are you doing this?"

"Taking a nap? Let me spell this out for you. I am *t-i-r-e-d*."

"No, Layla. Why are you acting like this? Why are you treating me this way? Why are you staying up all night talking to Chiara, but you won't talk to me?"

"God. You're such a baby."

I know why you said this. You know it's what stings the most. It's one of the few things that ever sent me crying to Mom or Dad.

And guess what? I'm not a baby. In fact, standing in your doorway, I felt like I'd aged years. I could see the mistakes you were making like I was looking in a rearview mirror. Why couldn't you see things the same way?

I took a deep breath.

"Layla. I love you." I tried to stay cool, but my eyes filled with tears. My voice cracked.

All your hard edges disappeared. You grabbed my wrist, pulled me into your room, and closed the door.

"Shhhhhhh," you said. Soothing or admonishing me?

We sat down on your bed. I kicked off my Uggs. You waited for me to say something. Our knees touched. I wanted to crawl under your comforter. I wanted everything else to go away. To tap my heels together three times and be back home again where life was simpler.

"So is it all true?" I asked finally.

You sighed. "Of course not."

Before the relief could reach my stomach, you said, "It's so much more complicated than that."

HERE'S WHAT YOU SAID NEXT:

Everything we hear is an opinion, not a fact. Everything we see is a perspective, not the truth.

You know I like quotes. I've memorized the good ones. I have shelves full of books I've desecrated with garish highlighters.

There are many arenas in which you outshine me, Layla, but when it comes to literature and loving the way words knock into each other, I have the upper hand. Are you the one who keeps a notebook in your bedside drawer where you write down all your favorite lines? I don't think so.

Yet there you were, spouting Marcus Aurelius like you did that sort of thing all the time.

No, of course I'd never heard that before, but I recognized that those words were not your own. I looked it up later on PretentiousQuotations.com or whatever, and there it was. But you were quoting someone else quoting someone else. Isn't that right?

Well, then how come when I bust out with some of my favorite lines you roll your eyes like: *Nell. She's such a nerd.* But when Mr. B. hit you with the Aurelius (let's face it: there's no way Schuyler or Liv knew that quote, and don't even get me started on Chiara) you were probably like: *My hero.*

Okay. I get that this isn't the point. I'd probably turn to mush too if someone I adored—someone like Sam, say—spouted off some Plato or even some John Lennon, so, yeah, *Judge not lest ye be judged* and all that. This sort of became my mantra. *Judge not,* especially when it's your sister, and your lives are intertwined.

Anyway, back to the Aurelius. Let's take it apart, shall we? *Everything we hear is an opinion, not a fact.*

Really? What about when Mr. Grandy, who is like the opposite of Mr. Barr because he's old, and his clothes are hideous and he doesn't know the first thing about contemporary music or anything after, like, the Second World War, what about when he says that the square root of 1,936 is 44. If I hear him say this, and I write it in my notebook, is it his opinion or is it fact?

It's fact.

Maybe you could argue that numbers aren't real, they're just a construct to express a concept, that a number is nothing more than a superspecific adjective, etc., etc., but I don't think that's what you were trying to tell me with Marcus Aurelius. You were trying to say something about how everyone has an opinion about everyone else but nobody knows what's true other than the person or people about whom that opinion is expressed.

Gossip isn't truth.

Duh.

You don't need to drag in a two-thousand-year-old Roman emperor to prove that. And anyway, what did you think I was doing in your room? I came to ask you about the truth, not about gossip. I came to ask you, the source, the object of the gossip: WHAT THE HELL IS GOING ON?

Everything we see is a perspective, not the truth.

People saw you downtown with Mr. Barr. I saw Mr. Barr on your laptop screen before you snapped it shut.

What is truth? What is not merely perspective? What, if anything, is fact?

"Just tell me," I said. "I can handle it. Tell me the truth."

You took both of my hands in yours. We faced each other, knees touching, like we were at a séance, or a meeting of the secret society of sisterhood.

"It's just like Madam Mai said. I'm in love. In real love."

You squeezed my hands. Hard. Nearly cracking bones. Aside from sore hands, what did I feel in that moment?

So many emotions.

You yawned. I'd recently learned in Life Sciences that yawning isn't so much about boredom or exhaustion—it helps cool the brain. I should have been the one yawning, because my head was on fire.

"I really do need that nap," you said.

"Yeah. Okay."

You leaned over and kissed my cheek.

"We'll talk more later?"

"Yeah, sure."

"I love you tons," you said.

"I know."

"And, Nell?"

"Yeah, I know."

"You do?"

"Of course."

"Promise?"

"Don't insult me."

I closed your door.

That's how I vowed to keep your secret.

I'M NOT SURE WHAT I can say about the miraculous friendship of Felix De La Cruz that I haven't already said, but when I walked from your room back to mine, my phone buzzed in my pocket.

Meet me on 24th St.?

When?

NOW.

Where?

U Know.

I grabbed my fleece and went to tell Dad I was going out, but he'd left for a bike ride. Since he couldn't do anything about losing his hair, Dad zeroed in on losing his belly flab.

"Did you have fun last night?" Sonia asked. If this were Mom, I'd know the subtext: *You better have had fun, because I spent an hour mopping whipped cream off the kitchen floor.* But this was sweet and easygoing Sonia, who just wanted to know if I'd had a good time.

"It was great."

"Is your homework all done?"

"Yep." Another lie.

"Well, then say hi to Felix."

He was waiting for me right where I knew he would be, in front of Happy Donuts. He handed me a maple glazed. Pitch-perfect Felix intuition.

"So?" he said.

I sat down on the bench clutching my donut. I wanted to devour it, the ultimate comfort food, but my stomach wasn't ready.

"Did you miss me?"

"Since yesterday?"

"No, I mean at your girls' party. Wasn't there a Felix-sized hole in your heart?"

"You mean an itty-bitty little hole?"

He shoved me. "Shut up. I'm massive. Feel these guns." He flexed his arm in front of me and I put my forehead down in the crook of his elbow.

"Uh-oh." He stroked my hair. "Tell Uncle Felix what's wrong."

I wanted to. God, did I want to. I wanted to share what you'd told me, spread the weight of it around. But promises are promises. Even unspoken ones.

"Too much pizza, not enough sleep."

"What about the nudity? Was there too much team nudity?"

"You're gross."

"In the immortal words of Professor Hubert J. Farnsworth: 'A man can dream.'"

"*Futurama?*"

"Season two, episode twenty. He's talking about the Finglonger—a glove with an extra-long index finger."

"Who doesn't need one of those?"

"I can't imagine." We leaned back against the front glass window of Happy Donuts. He put an arm around me. "So there was no team nudity."

"No, but there were some whipped-cream nipples."

"You're killing me, Nell."

"Is this what it's like?"

"What?"

"Being a boy. Do you just sit around all the time thinking about naked girls? Isn't there more to it?"

"Of course there is. We care about things like your intellect and your sense of humor and your capacity for kindness, but we also really like how you all look naked."

I sighed. "I'll never understand your gender."

"Is this about Sam?" he asked. "Do you still think he's Sam-azing? Are you still feeling Sam-ourous toward him? Or am I sensing some Sam-bivalence?"

"How long have you been working up that routine?"

"Just the walk over here."

"Cute."

"Then how come you didn't even crack a smile?"

"I don't know. I'm just . . ." I shook my head.

"Wow. Nell Golden at a loss for words."

"Maybe I just need to eat my donut." I took a bite. It tasted like fryer grease.

Felix and I always went to Happy Donuts when things were dire, when nothing but 470 calories, 13 grams of fat, and 24 grams of carbohydrates could lift our spirits. And there was the matter of the little donut man on the bag with his white-gloved hands, baker's cap, and smile. An anthropomorphized donut. How can that *not* cheer you up?

So how did Felix know? How did he know I needed the unmatched magic of Happy Donuts right at that very minute? Why had he texted me?

Meet me on 24th St.?

Even Felix, with all his intuitive powers, couldn't have known that you'd just dropped a nuclear bomb on me. That was when it occurred to me that Felix must have needed Happy Donuts for himself.

Something was wrong in Felixville.

Why was I such a shitty friend? That was the real question.

"Hey." I turned to face him. I wiped some chocolate from the corner of his mouth. "How are *you*?"

"Very well, thank you. And how are you this fine afternoon?"

"Seriously, Felix. Tell me. What's wrong?"

He sighed. "I don't even want to say it out loud." He looked down into his lap and crumpled the donut bag in his fist. "You know how talking about something makes it real? And sometimes just pretending it's not happening . . . you can fool yourself into believing it's not?"

I knew exactly what he meant. Exactly.

I checked his profile. Was he being serious? Or was he about to bust out with something like: *I'm gay,* which for the record, I'd totally be fine with, but is so obviously not true.

Nope. I could see it in his body. In his half-eaten donut. This was no joke.

"It's my dad, Nell."

I knew exactly what he was going to say next. Exactly.

I've always had my suspicions about Angel De Le Cruz, figured there was no way he could live up to his name. I don't mean to sound like a cynic, but you can't put a man with Angel's looks into a class of college girls year after year and not expect him to eventually fall under the spell of one of his students. And what about that whole romantic routine? The way Angel always calls Julia, Felix's mom, *el amor de mi vida?* "The love of my life." Or *mi corazón, mi alma?* "My heart, my soul." How can that be for real?

I sat fuming. Men. Teachers. What's wrong with the world?

"He's sick," Felix said.

"Oh, shit."

"Yeah. That about sums it up."

"How sick?"

" 'It is not, nor it cannot come to good.' "

Hamlet. Act 1 scene 2. No Fakespeare.

I took his hand. "Felix."

"It's in his adrenal cortex. I didn't even know he had an adrenal cortex."

He threw his donut into the trash bin and sat up straight,

filling his lungs with a big breath of air. "They say it's just a spot. A few centimeters in diameter. And there are treatments. And Dad is strong. And we're made of fight, we don't give up easily, it's a family trait, but I just feel like crawling into a hole and dying first."

"You can't. I wouldn't let you."

"I'm bigger than you. I'll shove you out of the way."

"It's just a spot, Felix. A few centimeters." This was lame, but I didn't know what else to say. I just hugged him.

I adored Angel. And Julia. I envied Felix, whose mother and father were married to each other and loved each other. That's probably why I'd told myself that Angel's grand proclamations couldn't be trusted. It was easier to believe that than the truth.

I took off my fleece. Too warm for November. The sky was thick and beige and I couldn't tell if it was about to rain or if maybe miles below its surface the earth was about to shift, and the shaking would throw us both from this bench.

I looked up the block, half expecting to see the Creed brothers—it felt like that kind of weather, the kind of afternoon when maybe the dead could rise and saunter down the street.

IT WAS ALL TOO MUCH for one day. But I came back from 24th Street and we packed our things and returned to Mom's and got our homework in order and chose our outfits for school and hit up Mom for lunch money. We had soccer finals coming up and I had play rehearsals and there were quizzes to study for, because life wants to be lived. You can't just sit on a bench all day outside a donut shop, wishing everything were different.

You and I didn't say another word about Mr. B. There were so many things I wanted to ask you on Sunday evening: Is this what you imagined that day on the sidewalk outside Madame Mai's when you twirled around like a foolish little girl? That you'd love a teacher? A man who had a reputation when it came to his students? But I also didn't want to talk about it anymore. Like Felix said, sometimes talking about things makes them real.

Mom homed in on my mood. She eyed me across the living room, where I sat trying to read the last chapter of *The Good Earth*. This should have been my sweet spot, but I couldn't focus.

"'When something is wrong with my baby,'" she said, "'something is wrong with me.'"

"I'm not a baby."

"Those are song lyrics, Nell."

"Well, that's a stupid song."

She went back to the Sunday paper and let me be.

I had Intro to Visual Arts Mondays third period.

I thought about skipping, going to that café near the park for a mocha latte or maybe sitting in a stall in the second-floor bathroom. Anything to keep my distance. But I went to class, dutiful as ever.

I felt queasy; when I entered, the art room seemed distorted. A few degrees off its axis. I managed to find my way to my drafting table and sat down next to Sean Black. He smiled and said, "'Sup, Nell?"

Mr. B. is having an affair with my sister. It's not just a rumor. It's real this time. Oh, and did I mention that my best friend's dad has cancer? Can I borrow a pencil?

I just shrugged.

I watched Mr. Barr for any sign of anything having shifted, and I felt pretty certain that he had no idea you'd told me. Did he even know how close we are? Did he worry we'd talk? Did he warn you not to tell me?

He caught my eye. He thought I was staring because I was paying attention.

"So, Nell, which is it?"

"Um . . . which is what?"

"Is *Piss Christ* by Andres Serrano a 'deplorable, despicable display of vulgarity' or is it 'darkly beautiful, ominous, and glorious'?" He moved the pointer around the slide in circles. A crucifix soaking in the artist's own piss. Was he trying to divert my attention? "Who's right? The conservative senator from New York or the renowned art critic?"

He is great-looking, I'll give you that. Dark hair. Blue eyes. Red lips. Broad shoulders. Nice smile. I could go down the list and check off all the boxes in the handsome column.

"Um . . . I don't know?"

"That's a perfectly respectable answer. It's hard to pass judgment on work in its time, isn't it? So you're saying wait and see?"

I stared at a doodle on my drafting table. "Yeah, I guess."

"Excellent."

Mr. Barr removed his plaid flannel shirt and flipped to a new slide. He wore jeans and a black T-shirt that revealed his Dalí tattoo. The melting clock. Time is irrelevant? Age doesn't matter? I tried reading all I could into his inked skin until the screeching of chairs pushing backward snapped me out of it. I went on to my next class.

I found Felix in the cafeteria at the end of his lunch period while I was just starting mine. He was sitting with a girl I'd seen him talking to once or twice, a sophomore. I couldn't remember her name.

I didn't want to just walk over and ask about Angel. For one thing, it had been less than twenty-four hours, so there wasn't likely to be any change. For another, Felix was clearly working on his game.

I approached anyway, to say hi and let him know with a look that he hadn't left my thoughts.

He kissed me on the cheek, using me to make this girl jealous, but I didn't mind. Much.

"Nell . . . Andie. Andie . . . Nell." He looked back and forth between us. "Best friend . . . girl I'd like to date. Girl I'd like to date . . . best friend."

Andie blushed and swatted his arm.

"Sorry. Is *girl* demeaning? Do you prefer *woman*?"

She laughed and walked off with her tray.

He turned to me. "You think *girl I'd like to date* was too much?"

"How about *girl I'm trying desperately to get into the pants of*?"

"It ends with a preposition. That's a deal breaker."

He piled all the dishes and napkins from the table onto his tray, not only his mess, but the stuff less-thoughtful students had left behind. That's Felix for you.

"You okay?" I asked. At that moment Mom's lyrics came back to me. *When something is wrong with my baby . . .*

"Hanging in. Staying positive."

"You sure? Anything I can do?"

"Yes. Continue to act as my foil whilst I pursue the fairer sex."

"Is that what I am?"

"You make me look better than I deserve." He smiled at me. "You're the very best foil a boy could ask for."

I watched him walk away, and in that moment, much as I love you and Mom and Dad, I wanted to live in a world with a population of two: me and Felix De La Cruz.

Play rehearsal was the beacon guiding me through the rest of my day. I could give you some bullshit about how inhabiting a different character might take me out of my own perplexing life, but honestly, I was seriously psyched to see Sam.

I didn't wait for him to approach me. I walked right over and took the empty seat next to him in the theater. Felix hadn't arrived yet, so I found the courage from someplace else.

"Hey there, Nell. Great game on Saturday. You killed it." He put his hand up for a high five.

"Thanks, Sam." I slapped his palm but then held on. Gave his hand a squeeze. Then two more. He wouldn't have known our family's secret code—three squeezes = *I love you*. And that's not even what I meant, because I didn't love Sam, but I wanted to find out if I could love him someday.

Why was I so bold? Touching him like that? Sending a convoluted signal? I guess I figured all bets were off. If Felix could tell a girl he hardly knew that he'd like to date her, if you could have Mr. B., if that wasn't just some silly schoolgirl fantasy, then maybe I could have a boy like Sam Fitzpayne.

When someone gives you the three squeezes, you squeeze

back twice: *How much?* Then that person squeezes your hand as hard as she can, to let you know that she loves you with every ounce of strength she can muster. That's the family code. Remember your favorite joke? You'd squeeze three times: *I love you.* I'd squeeze back twice: *How much?* Then you'd let your hand go limp in mine and laugh.

I laughed too, but honestly, that always broke my heart just a little bit.

Sam looked at me. *What's with you today?* He had a mischievous glint in his eye. I liked getting looked at that way, having my layers peeled back.

"HAMLET!" Ms. Eisenstein bellowed.

"Bummer. Gotta go."

We'd starting costume fittings, and Sam disappeared backstage to return in tights that didn't leave much to the imagination.

"Holy Banana Hammock!" Felix whispered. He'd taken Sam's seat. "There is no way in hell I'm getting into a pair of those. No way." We both stared.

"I don't get it," I said. "I thought this was *Hamlet* in a San Francisco high school? So what's with the Elizabethan getup?"

"Clearly Ms. Eisenstein just wants to see Sam's junk."

"Or maybe she's having some fun with, uh . . . anachronism?"

"Or . . . maybe *you* want to have some fun with *Sam's* anachronism," Felix said. "Especially after seeing him in those tights!"

Not really. I didn't think about things like that. It's sort of hard to admit, but what I wanted was the *spin-around-on-*

the-sidewalk-to-music-that-isn't-playing-with-a-grin-as-wide-as-a-freeway kind of crazy love. Stupid, huh? Naive? I mean, after everything I've seen with Mom and Dad, and everything I knew about what happens with most kids, especially in high school. Still: I wanted real love. I wanted what I saw in your eyes, even if I worried that what gave you that look was wrong.

"What's with that girl, Felix?" I asked.

"What girl?"

"Andie? The one you'd *like to date?*"

He sighed. "I don't know. She's cute. I need distraction. Hazel Porter doesn't know I exist and you're in love with a man in tights. What do you expect me to do?"

I nudged him with my knee. It was an old joke that Felix only bothered with other girls because I wasn't available to him, but we both knew that our bond was different and would never be romantic. There were times, though, when I wondered if maybe we had it all figured out. That maybe we were in the midst of the best that love can offer.

"She likes you. I can tell."

"And Sam likes you."

"You're just saying that because of what I just said."

"Nope. This ain't a quid pro quo. And if you need proof, just look at his tights."

"Jeez, Felix. Obsess much?"

When rehearsal ended I took my time packing up my stuff. Felix bolted so he could meet his parents for dinner. After my earlier move with Sam, I wanted to see if I could sit back and wait. See if maybe he'd come to me.

"Hey, Nelly G."

I liked that. I liked that a lot.

"Hey, Sam."

He reached for my backpack. "May I take your bag?"

"Um, sure."

He walked me out to the street in front of school.

"Your ride here yet?"

"If you mean the number forty-three bus, then no."

"The bus? After dark? A young girl like you?"

I shrugged.

"Not on my watch." He slung my backpack over his shoulder and reached for my hand. "I'm driving you home."

Any other day I'd have said no or called to get permission. I know the rule. No getting in a car driven by someone not known to Mom or Dad. When Mom was a teenager in suburban Chicago, four kids from her high school died in a car accident. The driver wasn't drinking or using drugs, she was just a seventeen-year-old taking her friends home from school. Maybe the music was on too loud. Maybe she was distracted by something that happened that day. Who knows? But because of this tragedy some forty years ago, I'm not allowed to get in a friend's car unless Mom has given this friend the third degree, like it would make any difference. Accidents happen. That's why they're called accidents.

But I didn't call Mom because it wasn't any other day; it was the day after you'd confirmed that you were in love with your art teacher, so I figured hitching a ride with Sam amounted to a pretty minor infraction of Golden rules and regulations.

"It's not too far out of your way?" I asked.

"I don't even know where you live, but wherever it is, it's not out of my way."

We walked two blocks to a parking lot. The daily rate was twenty dollars. And you wonder why Mom and Dad won't buy you a car?

He drove a Mini. Like he wasn't already adorable enough. Put that boy behind the wheel of a burnt-orange Mini Cooper with a black-and-white checkered roof? And then have him go and open the door for me?

Forget about it: I was done.

The bus ride home always feels like it lasts a lifetime, but the drive with Sam went way too quickly. We took Masonic and drove through the Presidio. Sam unrolled our windows so we could smell the eucalyptus. What boy cares about smelling nature? How did he know how much I loved that stretch of road with its tall, wondrous, dying trees?

"Do you know about the Goldsworthy?" he shouted over the music and the rushing air from the open windows.

"Nope."

"Andy Goldsworthy has an installation, *Wood Line,* in that grove right there." He pointed to his left. "We came on a field trip for Mr. B.'s sculpture class. It's awesome. You can walk on it."

"Sounds cool." I tried not to betray the distress caused by the mention of Mr. B.'s name.

"I'll take you sometime."

"I'd like that." *I'd like that?* What was I? A Shakespearean maiden? "I mean, that sounds like fun." I took in a deep breath of the medicinal, earthy eucalyptus. "How about now?"

"Now?" He looked over at me. "It's dark out."

I held up my phone. "There's an app for that!"

He pulled off Presidio Boulevard onto a side road, and parked.

"Don't you have to get home?"

I don't know where the boldness came from, really I don't. "Yes," I said. "But I'd rather walk on the Goldsworthy."

He looked at me. I pressed the flashlight app on my phone and shined it in his face. "What, are you afraid of the dark?"

We climbed out of the car and wandered into the eucalyptus grove. It was silent but for the sound of the cars on Presidio Boulevard and the dried leaves and twigs crackling under our shoes. A paved, lit walking path lay to our right. I'd been on it a few times with Dad. Dad is the type to always stop and read every sign aloud to us whether we're interested or not, so I knew that path was called Lovers' Lane because soldiers as far back as the 1800s took it from the army base to visit their wives or girlfriends in the city. I thought of mentioning this to Sam. Show him I knew things too. Even if I'd never heard of Goldsworthy, I knew about Lovers' Lane. But it was too flirty, even for the new, bolder me.

We found the art installation—a long, snaking line of logs fused together to look like one fallen tree, bending and curving impossibly through the forest. He hopped up and then motioned for me to step in front of him.

"Ladies first." He offered his hand.

I took it and he hoisted me up. I started walking, heel to toe, arms out wide, like I'd learned on the balance beam in SF Gymnastics all those years ago. I was never particularly poised in my hot-pink, too-small leotard, but on this night, in these woods, in front of the boy I adored, grace found me.

"It's ephemeral," Sam said.

I didn't respond. I didn't want to ruin what had become the most perfect moment of my life.

"This whole thing. It's going to disappear. It's art for only so long as it survives. Eventually the weather, erosion, rot, inconsiderate hooligans . . . something will ruin this and it'll all be gone."

Heel to toe. Heel to toe.

"That's . . . sad," I said.

"It's okay. It's not made to last."

I stopped in my tracks and Sam bumped into me from behind. He grabbed my waist to steady himself. I turned off my flashlight app, plunging us into darkness.

"What are you doing?"

"Preserving art." I switched on my camera. "Now it'll live forever. Smile."

I held the phone out in front of us and leaned back into Sam. He put his chin on my shoulder. I angled the viewfinder down so it would capture Sam and me and the winding sculpture behind us.

The flash blinded me. I leaned against him until I could see again. And then I continued to lean. He kept his head on my shoulder and I felt his breath on my neck while he clutched my waist, the thumb of his left hand gently rubbing my hip bone. It was like we were totally making out except I was facing the wrong way.

"Onward?" he whispered.

I turned the flashlight app on again and lit up what remained, another twenty yards. I took a step away.

When we reached the end of *Wood Line,* we hopped off and turned around. I was ready to navigate it back downhill, hoping for something else to draw our bodies together, but he started out of the grove of trees toward the path.

Once on the fabled Lovers' Lane he picked up his pace; a few times we separated to allow a jogger or a dog walker between us.

We were back at his car in two minutes.

"It's late," he said. "I'd better get you home."

We rode home in silence. I could still feel where his thumb had caressed my hip bone. There was a passenger with us, a new presence squeezed in between our seats. Something was happening with Sam and me.

Mom was already in the kitchen. You were in your room with your door closed.

"Thank God you're here." Mom handed me a cucumber and a knife. "I can never get these as perfectly thin as you do."

No questions about why I was late. How I got home. If I'd broken any rules.

I put my backpack down, reached into the cabinet above

the stove, and grabbed the mandoline. I started running the cucumber over the blade, and as the paper-thin strips piled up, Mom looked at me with wonder.

"What is that? Who are you? How did you learn all this? When did you grow up?" She reached over and smoothed my hair. "Last time I checked you were wearing a princess costume and talking with a lisp."

I shrugged. "Shit happens."

Mom sighed and rolled her eyes. "Language, Nell."

She picked up my backpack and hung it on the hook she'd put in the closet door for that very purpose.

Here's what it took for me to surprise and astonish our mother: slicing cucumbers with a mandoline I'd bought with money she'd left for takeout. What if she knew what you were doing?

"Go get your sister. Tell her it's time to climb out of her cave and come to dinner. Honestly. Why do they have to give you girls so much homework?"

"They don't."

"You're right. They don't. I never got that much home-work and look at me." She gestured around the chef's kitchen she barely knows how to use.

What I meant: *They don't give us that much homework; Layla pretends she's overworked to hide her secrets.*

I knocked. I'd learned.

"Come in."

I cracked the door open only enough for you to hear me.

"Dinner's ready."

"Come on in."

You had your easel out and your acrylics. Half a psyche-delic landscape made its way across your canvas.

"Mom thinks you're doing homework."

"I am, silly. This *is* my homework."

"Oh."

"How was rehearsal?"

"Sam drove me home."

"Sam Fitzpayne?"

I nodded.

"You're not supposed to get into cars with boys."

"Yeah, and there are things you're not supposed to do either, so . . ."

You didn't look up from your painting.

"I just want you to be careful. There's something about that Sam I don't trust. There's just a . . . subtle cruelness about him, or something."

I walked out of your room and slammed the door. I'd just had this magical moment, and all I wanted was for you to read this on my face and know that inside me bloomed my own psychedelic landscape.

Dinner was awkward. I'm sure Mom looked at me think-ing: *Moody teenager.* I sulked and pushed my food around my plate while you talked a mile a minute. You'd just read the most AMAZING poem for English Lit. You were studying Willem de Kooning; his art is INCREDIBLE. It's so AWESOME that we made it to the soccer finals, who cares if we win? Did either of us notice the sunset? It was GORGEOUS.

Your exuberance exhausted me.

Later, when I was lying in bed, you pushed open my door. You didn't knock.

Parker had just been telling me how guys don't rub girls' hip bones with their thumbs like that unless they totally like the girl. Duncan was a little more skeptical. Parker told him he didn't know anything because he was only fourteen and hadn't had enough experience. You interrupted us.

"Are you okay?"

I'd asked you that very question a hundred times over the last few months.

"Yeah."

"You seemed kind of . . . upset. Like, you didn't say a word at dinner."

"You didn't exactly give me an opportunity."

"What does that mean?"

"It means you were rambling on and on about how totally *amazing* everything is and how the sky is *beautiful* and whatever."

"So? I'm happy. Do you have a problem with that?"

I sighed. No. Of course I don't have a problem with that. I want you to be happy. There's little more I wish for in the world. But . . .

You came in and closed the door. You kicked off your slippers and climbed into my bed. You pulled the covers up over both of us.

"Layla."

"What?"

I wanted to say: *What about the other girls? Yelli Rothman?*

115

Hazel Porter? How do you know you aren't just the flavor of the month?

"Nothing."

You squeezed me and whispered, "You're my sister."

"I know."

"I love you more than anything."

"I know."

WE LOST.

You were right. It didn't much matter. We'd made the finals and that was enough. We played hard, or you and the team played hard and I kept the bench warm. At the final whistle the score was three to one.

Our opponents came from an all-girls' school. As I sat and watched, I did the math. They had three times the pool to choose from when putting together their team, so of course they were better than us. Plus it was a Jesuit school, so they probably had God on their side to boot.

I wondered what life would be like at St. Mary's. Wearing a uniform every day. No makeup. No boys who'd inspire you to try out for the play just to get closer to them. No boys to give you a ride home when it's dark outside. No Felix . . .

I bet their art teacher doesn't have tattoos. I bet he doesn't wear black jeans and tight T-shirts.

Maybe life would have been better at that school for us, but it was never an option. We weren't like those boys and girls in plaids and ties who clogged the streets at the top of Pacific Heights, navigating the entryways into their separate institutions. Our parents had different values. Different plans for us.

Why were we born to a couple of atheists? Why are Mom and Dad so aggressively progressive? Why do they always seek out bastions of liberalism?

Why do they always say things to us like: *We want you to be strong, independent women. We want you to speak your minds and demand that others listen. We want to give you the freedom to make the right decisions.*

Look at what can happen when you allow your daughters too much freedom. Would it have been so terrible if we'd been sent to a stricter school?

It's a stupid fantasy, I know. I don't really believe St. Mary's is the answer. We would have hated it. Probably would have gotten expelled. But from the bench, those girls looked happy. Strong. They played some kick-ass soccer, and I can't say for sure, but I doubt they had a teacher in the stands who'd showed up to cheer on his girlfriend.

There was a party that night. For juniors. A party with beer and boys and flirting, and Sam asked me if I was going and I said yes because you're a junior and I knew you'd take me with you. I knew you'd understand how important it was to me.

"I'd take you," you said, "if I had any intention of going, which I totally don't."

"Gee, thanks."

"If Sam asked you, why don't you just go with him?"

"Because he didn't ask me to *go with him*. He just asked if I was going."

I was wasting my breath; you understood. You'd been in high school two years longer than I had. Sam and I might have been beginning something, but we still stood outside the starting gates. He couldn't just offer to bring me. That's not how it's done.

"Well, you should go. Obviously he wants you there."

"You think?"

"Of course he does. He wouldn't have asked you if he didn't care."

"Really?"

You smiled. "Really."

"Cool."

"So you should go."

"Maybe I will."

"And we should pretend we're going together. That way Dad won't freak out."

Oh. So that's what the ego stroking was about. You just wanted me to cover for you so you could go off with Mr. B.

Dad did his standard *don't let her out of your sight* routine, and you promised you wouldn't, and we agreed we'd be home not a minute past 11:45—a fifteen-minute extension on our curfew.

Felix agreed to come with me. It didn't take much convincing. He was hoping for a shot at Hazel Porter.

"Do you think those rumors about her and Mr. B. were true?"

"Not a chance," he said.

"How do you know?"

"Because Hazel was going out with Gideon Banks last year. Sure, she spent lots of time with Mr. B., but that's because he was her adviser, and they became friends, and he's cool and she's the coolest. But it was never anything more than that."

"How did you become such an expert?"

"I do my research."

"Creeper."

"Guilty as charged."

The party was awful, and not because all parties are *stupid* and *boring* and *lame* like you'd become fond of saying, but because (1) Sam didn't show; (2) without you, I'm just a freshman, that's the sad truth. And, like the fortune cookie wisdom goes, bad things come in threes: (3) no fewer than five separate people came up to me and asked, *Where's your sister?*

They said it in that way that meant they had a pretty decent idea where you were. Eyebrows raised knowingly. *Wink. Wink. Nudge. Nudge.*

You get the picture.

Felix and I left after an hour. He'd had two beers; I'd had none. He didn't speak a word to Hazel. It felt like a Happy Donuts kind of night to me, but Felix lobbied for a *Simpsons* marathon at his house. *The Simpsons* always pulls me out of a funk, especially when viewed with Felix, who does dead-on impressions of the characters.

Felix reeked of beer.

"We need to buy you some gum."

"Por que?"

"Because you smell like a distillery."

"You mean I smell like baby food?"

True, there was a park we went to sometimes near the Anchor Brewing factory, and the dominant odor it gave off: Eau de Baby.

"I mean your parents will know you're drunk."

"I'm not drunk. And anyway, they have bigger fish to fry."

I grabbed his arm and we took turns pulling each other up the hill. It wasn't an Oh My God hill, but still, we needed the extra help.

"So. Where *is* she tonight? What's she up to?"

"I don't know."

"You always know. Your life's work is knowing what Layla is up to."

"Well, she isn't up to what everyone at that party thinks she's up to." I hated lying to Felix—it upset the natural order of the universe.

"That's because everyone at that party is a Cretan."

"An evil brute."

"A lazy glutton."

We'd learned The Cretan Paradox in our eighth-grade humanities class with Mr. Garcia. The Cretan poet Epimenides says, "All Cretans are liars." Because spoken by a Cretan, the statement is true if and only if it is false.

Discuss.

How I missed Mr. Garcia. Sixty-something Mr. Garcia with his ill-fitting Dockers and neck beard. Safe, unknowable Mr. Garcia.

Angel looked every bit the same to me. His hug was still all-consuming. He offered me a sandwich, like he always does, or a dish of ice cream, and like I always do, I agreed to let him fix me something I didn't really want.

He and Julia disappeared into the kitchen, and Felix and I went down to the basement to Felix's guy pad.

"He looks good," I said.

"He always looks good. Like father like son. But, you know, he hasn't started treatment yet, so . . ."

"When?"

"Soon. But first they have to make sure they know what they're dealing with, like, is it only in this so-called adrenal cortex, or is it other places too?" He shook his head, then lowered the lights. "How 'bout we start with a classic? Bart versus Australia."

"Season six. Episode sixteen."

"God, how I love you."

Just then Angel and Julia emerged with microwave s'mores, one of their specialties. "The flavor of camping without sacrificing the miracle of indoor plumbing," Angel liked to say.

Julia handed Felix his plate. "Finally you admit what we've all known for years."

"What are you talking about? I've never hidden my love for Nell."

I knew this was a joke, but still, I couldn't keep from blushing, which amused and delighted Angel. He loves to embarrass me. Once, early in my friendship with Felix, I'd tried out some of my fifth-grade Spanish and responded that I was *embarazada,* which actually means "pregnant," and now whenever I turn red Angel says, "Are you expecting?"

"Can Nell sleep over? We have, like, a thousand episodes to get through."

"Of course. She's always welcome," Julia said. She took Angel's hand and they started back up the basement stairs. "Just don't stay up all night."

"There. Done. You aren't leaving."

"I don't know, Felix."

"What?" He looked hurt. And of course I wanted to stay, but I wasn't sure how to handle you and the lie we'd told Dad about going to the party. We'd planned to meet on the corner at 11:40 so we could walk in the door together, but I wasn't about to ruin my night to protect your secret.

I texted you: *Staying at Felix's. Tell Dad the party was lame.*

In the middle of our third episode, the one where Homer and Marge tell the story of how they first met and fell in love, my phone rang. It was midnight.

Dad was pissed.

"I'm standing here with your sister and I'm noticing that you're not here with her."

"I know. I'm at Felix's. I'm going to stay here tonight."

"Is that so?"

Dad loves Felix. He loves Felix's parents. He never minds when we have sleepovers.

"What's the problem?"

"The problem, Nell, is that you wanted to go to a party with your sister, and against my better judgment I let you go, and then you fail to show up at the appointed hour, and I can't help but wonder why."

"Because . . . I went home with Felix."

"Are you drunk? Did you take any drugs?"

"What?"

"Let me talk to Angel or Julia. Are they home?"

"Of course they're home. Dad. Why are you being such a prick?"

I regretted it as soon as I said it. Dad is pretty loose about language, except when it's directed at him.

"Okay. That's it. I'm coming to get you."

"Dad. What did Layla tell you?"

"She said you thought the party was *lame,* which, by the way, is a word I'd like to see eradicated from both of your vocabularies. She said you left early with Felix."

"Dad." My eyes were stinging with tears. I felt six years old. I wanted to shout, *This isn't fair.* I wanted to shout, *I'm the good one.* I wanted to shout, *Punish her, not me.*

"I'll be there in five. Be ready."

Felix waited out on the steps with me. I'd started crying when I'd hung up and was doing my best to rein it in before Dad arrived. It was freezing. I sat one step down from Felix, in between his knees. He ran his hands up and down the sleeves of my denim jacket, but I couldn't stop shivering.

"Sorry this night has been such a big sack of poo."

I sniffled. "You're such a poet."

"First the man of your dreams stands you up, and then your dad starts acting like it's his time of the month."

"Maybe it is."

"Usually he's so chill. At least with me."

"I guess I should have asked him if I could sleep over."

"Can't hurt to ask."

Dad pulled up in his Porsche, and for the first time I thought he looked ridiculous in it. He looked the opposite of cool. He looked old and bald. And angry.

"Get in." And then, "Hi, Felix."

"Hi, Matthew."

"Say hello to your folks for me."

"They're sleeping."

"Well, then say hello in the morning."

We drove off without speaking a word to each other. I think you should know that in that silence I seriously considered telling Dad everything.

"You're only fifteen," he finally said. "I know you want nothing more than to be treated like an adult, but I can't treat you like an adult because you're my child, and I especially can't treat you like an adult when you change the rules without consulting me. You promised to be home at eleven-forty-five and you weren't. Case closed."

"Case closed?" I hate when Dad pulls his lawyer crap on me.

"Look, I worry about you, okay?"

"I guess I should have called."

"Of course you should have called."

"But you don't need to worry about me."

"Yes, I do."

I tried again. "You don't need to worry about *me*."

"Yes, I do."

I'm sure you were confused when I came home and went to my room and wouldn't talk to you. I was so angry. Everything felt so *unfair*. We were watching *cartoons*! Eating *s'mores*! How can you get more wholesome than that?

You knocked, you rattled the knob, but I wouldn't undo the lock. You pounded.

Let her in, Duncan said. *She probably wants to apologize.*

Let her in, Parker said, *and tell her how much it hurts that Sam didn't show up.*

More pounding.

You don't feel like yourself when you're mad at Layla or when she's mad at you. Let her in. You need her.

I didn't need you. I had the Creed brothers.

They looked at each other and then at me.

But . . . we're not real.

YOU KNOW THAT POSTER IN the science lab? Albert Einstein with the quote *The only reason for time is so that everything doesn't happen at once.* I'm not sure Einstein actually said this—maybe it just looks good under a picture of him with his insane hair—but I wanted to tell Einstein that sometimes time is of no use.

Everything in the world was happening at once. Every clock was ticking. Every radio station was playing. Someone had turned up the speed on the treadmill while I was still trying to walk.

The play was opening in four days. We were in the middle of finals. And you'd all but disappeared: always out, busy, lying to Mom and Dad. Like that time I convinced Mom you didn't mutter *bitch,* I covered for you, helped maintain the fiction that you were just working hard at school.

And, of course, there was Sam.

After our Goldsworthy trek, after asking me if I was going to be at the party, after rubbing my hip bone with his thumb, he barely acknowledged me.

"You said 'the play's the thing,'" I whispered to Felix. "But guess what? The play is this weekend and Sam is already over me. My window has closed. On my fingers."

We were sitting in the back of the theater, watching Sam. The scene where he tells Ophelia "Get thee to a nunnery," one of the only original lines Ms. Eisenstein kept in the play, before walking offstage and leaving her all alone. I knew exactly how Ophelia must have felt.

"Maybe he's just distracted. He has like a thousand lines. And he's a junior, so his grades actually count. Plus the tights might be cutting off oxygen to his brain."

"I'm supposed *to be* the distraction," I whined.

"I find you distracting," Felix said. "Like a fly or a gnat."

"Gee, thanks."

He knocked me on the chin. "Buck up. There's the cast party coming up. And it's at his house, so he has to show."

All this work. For three performances. Friday night, Saturday matinee, Saturday night. It hardly felt worth it. Especially for the five lines I had, two of which were only one word.

I guess I was sitting in the auditorium that day coming to terms with what the sensible part of me already knew—that life is a long series of anticlimaxes. Starting high school? Soccer finals? School play? Sam's thumb on my hip bone? So when the final performance of the play rolled around— I guess the joke was on me.

Every movie I'd seen, book I'd read, or bad made-for-TV movie I'd watched about a school play went something like this:

The heroine's life changes on the night of the play in one of the following ways.

A. The lead actress falls suddenly ill, so the heroine gets to live out her dream of being a star.

B. The shy heroine opens her mouth and sings like an angel when before she could only croak like a frog.

C. The boy the heroine adores finally confesses his love.

And it always ends with a standing ovation.

Well, Isabella Jones didn't fall suddenly ill, and anyway, I wasn't Ophelia's understudy. I can't sing; plus this *Hamlet* isn't a musical. You'd know these things if you'd been there on Saturday night.

But you weren't.

Maybe it's unfair of me to be upset. After all, you did come on opening night, but lots of people's families came to all three performances.

Anyway, that leaves the evening with only one other cliché:

C. The boy the heroine adores finally confesses his love.

The play went off without a hitch. Felix got the biggest laugh of the night. There was thunderous applause but no standing ovation unless you count Hugh Feldman, who stood up to cheer for his girlfriend, Ava Price.

Backstage there was a ton of hugging and high fives and bouquets flying this way and that. There was sweat and smeared makeup and some serious BO. It was exciting. Exhilarating. Democratizing—it didn't seem to matter what part you played, how many lines you had, the fun was equal opportunity.

And: Sam kissed me on the lips.

To be totally honest, I could have been anyone. He spun me around and planted one—quick and delicious—then turned and threw an arm around Austin Baker's neck, pulling him in for a noogie.

Dad and Sonia were there. Mom made the matinee. Maybe it would have been less disappointing if you'd just told me you had no intention of coming, but you said you'd *try*.

Backstage cleared quickly, the odor retreating with the cast. Everyone had gone to the lobby to find their friends and family, and I suddenly realized that I didn't know where or when the party started or how I was going to get there.

But then I found Felix with Angel and Julia, Dad and Sonia. Thank God for Felix. I should make a bumper sticker and a T-shirt and maybe get it tattooed on my wrist. *Thank God for Felix.*

"You made everyone laugh," I said. "That's not easy to do. You did it. You brought your flair."

He turned to Dad. "There's a cast party downtown. Can I take Nell with me? And would it be okay if she slept over after so that I don't have to worry about her getting home safely?"

"Of course." Dad looked at me. *See? I can be reasonable. All you have to do is ask.*

"Thanks, Dad." I gave him a kiss on the cheek, and then, because I was still on a high from the play and feeling generous, I kissed Sonia too.

Angel and Julia drove us to Sam's party. We stopped first at the new retro burger place and slipped into a red vinyl booth. I ordered mine without onions or pickles.

"You love onions," Felix said.

"Not really."

He raised an eyebrow. "Someone has big plans tonight."

I turned red. Angel smiled a half smile at me. "Look at Nell. She's expecting again!"

Our burgers came to the table. Five for the four of us. Angel took the extra one, cut it in fours, put it in the middle. "Table burger!"

Angel ate his burger and the extra all on his own. Felix and I shared a smile. He had his appetite. That could only be counted as a good sign. I crossed my fingers under the table and made a wish for his adrenal cortex—that the spot lived there and only there.

Do you ever have those moments, Layla, when you know you're supposed to be enjoying yourself? When you tell yourself you're happy, having fun, but there's something gnawing at you? I guess that pretty much describes my life since I started to understand what was happening with you. I sat in that cool new burger joint, surrounded by people I love, while this monologue ran in my head:

Don't think about it. Don't think about it. Life is good. Life is great. You're on your way to a party with the boy you adore, who just kissed you on the lips. Don't think about Angel and the spots. Don't think about Layla and what she's doing. Life is good. You are with your best friend. On your way to a party. Don't think about it. Don't think about it.

Sam lives in a huge industrial loft with 360-degree views of the city. I've never been in any place like it. I thought people lived like this only on TV dramas about lawyers.

Inside the gigantic elevator Felix said, "Relax." His voice echoed off the steel walls. "This is supposed to be a celebration. You look like you're getting marched to the gallows."

"This may be my last chance."

"Drama queen!"

"No, I mean the play is over. I have no reason to talk to Sam. We'll probably never see each other again."

"Nell, our school has like five people in it. You'll see him again whether you want to or not."

The doors opened into the loft and there he stood, barefoot, holding a glass and smiling like he'd been doing nothing all night but waiting for the elevator to deliver me.

"You made it," he said.

"I made it."

"I'm glad."

Felix pinched my elbow: *Told you so,* and then disappeared.

Sam leaned over to kiss me on the cheek, smelling of tequila.

"You were great." I'd already said this to him backstage, but I wasn't sure he'd heard.

"Thanks. You too."

Generous, but untrue. I was simply there, like scenery.

"Do you want a drink?"

I didn't have to go back to Dad and his nose, so I said yes. I don't like to drink, you know this, but I also don't like to look like a loser. Cue the cheesy teen movie. *The Girl Who*

Drank to Impress the Boy. Sometimes you have to follow the script.

He poured me tequila over ice, added some sort of juice, and squeezed a lime into it. I hated it. I grabbed what was left of the lime and tried to get more out of it, then threw the whole thing in my cup. Not much help.

You can imagine the scene. Loud music, but bearable. Funk, not techno. Huddles of friends like an archipelago scattered across the living room. Some whispering, some yelling. Laughter. Rehashing of the play's best moments, already distant memory. White walls. Framed black-and-white photographs of famous people from the sixties I couldn't identify. Those few sips of tequila prickling sweet and sour beneath my skin. Beyond the floor-to-ceiling windows, the lights of a city I loved twinkled like jewels underwater.

I felt happy. Like Sam said: I'd made it.

We walked around together. Sam offered to refill drinks. I complimented people on their performances.

"Is it hot in here?" Sam asked, his face adorably flushed. I thought it felt perfect, like when you slip into water that matches your body temperature. I'd finished most of my drink.

"Maybe a little."

"I'm going to get a T-shirt." He grabbed my hand. "Come with me."

Here's the thing about lofts. They're open and exposed and even the staircase doesn't have walls, so as we went up it we could be seen by the whole party.

His room faced east with a full view of the Bay Bridge. I

stood with my nose pressed to the glass. It was colder than I'd expected.

"Nice view."

He came up behind me. Close enough for me to feel him, but without any parts of us touching.

"It's even better with you in it."

He slipped his arms around my waist and started kissing the back of my neck. He pressed his body against me, hard enough that I worried we'd both go flying out that window, in slow motion, with twenty-four floors to fall, like in an action movie.

He pulled my sweater over my head. I had on a tank top and he quickly pulled that off too. I think I gasped from surprise. Everything was happening all at once.

This was what I wanted. It was what I'd wanted since the first day I saw him in the hall at City Day, since I first saw that one dimple—I wanted him to want me, I wanted him to want me more than you.

He took my hand and moved me to his bed. He unbuttoned his shirt, threw it on the floor, fell down on top of me. We kissed like that, skin on skin, for not nearly long enough. I'd have been happy to spend my night just like that. I didn't need, didn't want anything more.

Then he started fumbling with the buttons on my jeans.

I took his hand and moved it away. He cocked his head and squinted at me in a way I'm sure he knew was endearing. He reached out and stroked my hair. "Nell."

"Yeah?"

"Nell," he said again. "Nell Golden. Nelly G."

How could I not love the way he said my name?

"You know I like you, right?"

"I guess so."

He laughed. "I thought it was obvious."

"I can be sort of dim sometimes." I don't even know why I said that. What I meant was that it's hard for me to believe someone like him could be interested in someone like me.

He laughed again and kissed me. God, his lips were so soft. He took his index finger and he traced it from my chin down my bare chest to the first button on my jeans. He looked at me and smiled. *Please?*

I sighed.

Must I tell you everything that happened? Every detail? Fair is fair, and I don't ask what happens when you find yourself pressed against Mr. B., so I'll keep this to myself.

I don't know how long we'd been gone, but when I came back downstairs nobody seemed to notice, unless you count Felix who looked at me as if I'd just returned from the war.

"God," he said. "Where were you? Duh. Obvious. But God. Did you have to be up there so long? I was worried."

"What were you worried about?"

"You drank tequila."

"So?"

"Tequila is an angry mistress."

"I didn't even finish it."

"You're all flushed."

"So?"

"Can we leave now? We can get back to our *Simpsons* marathon."

I looked around but didn't spy Sam. In the kitchen? "I don't know."

"What do you mean you don't know? Do you want to leave?"

"I don't know."

I really didn't. What's the right way to exit a party after you've been, you know, *intimate* with the host? If you'd been there, you'd have told me what to do. For one of the first times, I felt like I couldn't be totally honest with Felix, but why? You probably could have explained that too, and then, I just started to hate Mr. B. for taking you away from me.

"I need another drink."

"No, you don't. What you need is Season two, episode twenty: 'The War of The Simpsons,' in which Homer gets drunk at a party and embarrasses Marge."

"I'm embarrassing you?"

"Not yet. But we should leave."

I scanned the room. No Sam. "Maybe *you* should leave."

He took a step away, stung. "I told your dad I'd take you home."

"You're not in charge of me, Felix."

Why? Why? Why?

Why was I acting this way? Hurting the person I loved?

And where was Sam? I still had hope that something great was beginning. The way he'd smiled at me. The way he'd said my name . . .

But I couldn't see him anywhere, and he hadn't held my hand on the way back down the stairs.

"I can't leave here without you," Felix said, and he walked off to join a cluster of cast members.

I followed him. "Fine. I'll leave. But I want to go home. To my home."

"Which one?"

He knew we spent our weekends at Dad's, so I couldn't help but take this as a dig. He had one home; I had two.

"Wait here." I went to find Sam in the kitchen. I couldn't leave without saying good-bye. I didn't *want* to leave without saying good-bye. I wanted to kiss him, out in the open. If this was the start of my spin-around-on-the-sidewalk real love, then it should begin with a kiss in public.

He was standing with a group of guys, about to take a shot of tequila, lime in one hand, shot glass in the other.

"I'm leaving," I said.

He gave me the finger the *just wait a second* one. He threw back his head and drank, put the lime wedge in his teeth, and slammed the glass on the table. He waved me closer.

Then he put his hand up for a high five.

I gave him a quick slap and turned to go, hoping he'd say *wait* or *aren't you forgetting something* or *where's my kiss?*

"Later," he called after me.

Felix stood by the elevator. We don't fight. I don't know the angry Felix, this boy with stiff posture and robot face. I wanted to apologize—try to explain my crippling confusion, but instead I linked my arm in his. He disentangled himself.

We got a cab immediately. He gave the driver Dad's address.

"Well, I guess you got what you wanted," he said, not unkindly.

"I guess."

"I told you it would happen."

I looked out the window. A late-night fog was rolling in, and the streets looked postapocalyptic. I didn't want to talk. I didn't want to tell him about what happened. I wanted to sit and watch the city go by outside my window, and because Felix is my best friend, he didn't say another word to me until the cab pulled up in front of Dad's.

He waved off my attempt to give him some cash. "Good night."

"Call me tomorrow?"

"Sure."

"Felix?"

"Yeah?"

"You did great tonight. You made everyone laugh."

"I know, you already told me that."

Dad wasn't surprised to see me. If he's learned anything having teenagers, it's that plans change minute by minute.

"Good times?" he asked.

I nodded and yawned. "Good times," I said, dodging his nose by making a beeline to my room. I took off my shoes and tiptoed past your door, but you have supersonic hearing. You poked your head out and gave me that look: *So?*

"You missed the final performance."

"I know. Sorry." You shrugged. "C'mon. Tell me about the party."

"The party was a celebration of the final performance that you missed."

You rolled your eyes and closed your door.

I went to my room and crawled under the covers. I wanted nothing but silence. Blankness. White noise. I didn't want voices: Parker's, Duncan's, yours, Felix's, Sam's, my own. I wanted to feel without thinking. Sleep without dreaming.

I wanted to twinkle underwater like the lights of the city.

WINTER BREAK.

Felix and his parents went to Mexico City to visit family. The doctors, having determined that his cancer hadn't spread, cleared Angel to take a trip before the operation to remove his adrenal glands. Everyone else we knew went off skiing in Tahoe or surfing in Hawaii. We weren't going anyplace because Sonia was waist-deep in trial prep. It was Dad's Christmas this year, and he decided that we'd stay home and watch her work.

I was dreading two weeks alone with you.

But we had a great time.

Maybe our last great time.

I slept through half of that Sunday and woke to the memory of Sam's hands on my body. All things considered, it's not a bad way to wake up. A decent sleep, four glasses of water, several trips to the bathroom to pee out that tequila, a text from Felix with an *xoxo,* and I got what I'd hoped for: a better outlook on the previous night. After all, Sam had held my hand on the way *up* the stairs.

I found you in your room, flat on your back, staring at the ceiling, throwing a soccer ball in the air and catching it, over and over again. After so many weeks of Chirpy Layla, I was surprised to see Glum Layla.

"I'm sorry I didn't make it to the final performance," you said. "It's just that George left this morning for New York. It was my last chance to see him." I sat down at your desk. "You understand, don't you?"

I nodded, just trying to swallow the *George*-ness.

"Look. He gave me this." You reached under your covers and removed an enormous book. *Mark Rothko: The Works on Canvas.* You caressed the spine, ran your fingers over the front of it. "Isn't it beautiful?"

"It's a book."

"We saw the show together."

"Right."

"Did you know most of Rothko's paintings are untitled?"

"No, I can't say I knew that."

You smiled knowingly. "Some things defy definition."

I tried not to gag. You placed the book back under your comforter and resumed tossing the soccer ball.

"Now, will you tell me about the party? Pretty please?"

"There's not much to tell. It was a party. Lots of people were there. Oh, and I hooked up with Sam."

You threw the ball at me and I ducked. It barely missed your precious laptop.

"Oh my God."

"I know."

"Now what?"

That was the million-dollar question.

"Now we get a two-week break from each other."

"He's going away?"

I just looked at you. Of course he was going away.

"So I guess it's just you and me, kid."

"And Dad, Sonia, and her briefs."

"Gross."

"Not her *underwear,* idiot," I said. "Her *legal* briefs."

Even Mom was abandoning us for the holiday to spend it with Gramma and Gramps in suburban Chicago. I guess I'll never really understand how Mom and Dad strike their deals. But if anyone had asked, I'd have said I preferred to go with Mom. I wouldn't even have minded the bitter cold or the soulless suburbs. There's just something about being around Gramma that's *normal.* Gramps is another story—he's a man of few words, like . . . three—but somehow he makes Gramma happy.

Can you imagine it? Christmas in their condo with nothing to do but play Chinese checkers, look at old pictures, and watch the nightly news? With nothing to eat but stale hard candies, Wasa crackers, and those triangle cheeses? Sure, there would be museum trips and visits to the beauty parlor so Gramma can have someone else blow-dry her hair, and maybe a meal or two in a nice restaurant. But when we're around Gramma and Gramps we're *the grandchildren* or *the grandkids* or *the girls,* and I guess what I'm saying is I wouldn't have minded being treated like a child for a little while, even if it wasn't skiing in Tahoe or surfing in Hawaii.

After watching TV all day Monday, I woke up Tuesday and went for a run. I'd barely moved my body since the soccer finals. You were still in bed.

Don't you wish you'd gone skiing? Duncan asked.

Don't you wish you'd gone to Hawaii? Parker echoed.

They were suffering a bit of the stuck-at-home-with-nothing-to-do blues too.

Where did he go for break? Duncan asked.

I didn't know. Maybe nowhere.

Why don't you just give him a call? You know you want to.

I didn't have his number.

Duh. It's in the student handbook. So is his email. You can text him. There's a whole world of communication opportunities open to you.

As we ran through Twin Peaks, even on the climb up, they never got short of breath. Running, like everything else they ever did, seemed effortless.

Parker turned around and started jogging backward. *You know, you should probably talk to her. Find out what's going on. You can't keep acting like nothing is happening.*

I grunted. The upward climb was doing a number on my lungs.

What are you afraid of?

I was afraid of everything.

Take control, Duncan said. *Don't be passive. Call Sam—you deserve to know what's going to happen next. And talk to Layla about Mr. B. Start being a better sister.*

In the end, I took 50 percent of the Creed brothers' advice. I didn't call Sam, but I did talk to you. Well, I took maybe 70 percent of their advice, because though I didn't call Sam, I did send him a text.

An innocuous, safe text. Totally un-creeper-like.

How's UR break? Hope UR somewhere fun. ☺

I worked it over and over in my head on the last stretch of my run. With all that planning, I could have come up with something more clever. But I didn't want clever. I wanted natural. I wanted off-the-cuff. I wanted *you're barely on my mind.*

He didn't text back.

Later, you suggested that maybe he'd gone to Europe. The Caribbean. Someplace where the roaming charges were so high he'd left his cell at home. That was kind of you, Layla, since you didn't believe it. You were just trying to make me feel better. And for those two weeks it worked.

But first, we needed to warm up to each other. We needed to reach the place where I could admit I'd texted Sam and heard nothing back, and you could tell me about the perfect version of love you'd stumbled into, all of which meant I'd have to meet you where you were. Put aside my better judgment and just listen.

That first Wednesday of break I convinced you to leave the house and your laptop—the holy temple of messaging and video-chatting—so that I could introduce you to my favorite café.

We took the same bus we took to school, but it felt different, changed, like going back to visit a place you went when you were younger, or a theater when all the lights come back on. We walked by City Day. The gates were locked. A poster advertising *Hamlet* still hung in the glass case. I brushed off the memory of searching in vain for your face in the audience on closing night. The memory of Sam kissing me on the lips backstage, quickly, like an accident. There was something more exciting about that kiss than the kissing that happened later in his bedroom.

I turned, leading us up a different block from the one Felix and I usually take to the café. I wanted a fresh start. A vacation.

I ordered for us. *Two mocha lattes, please.* I smiled at the waiter who'd served me countless times and he smiled back, but I could see that he had absolutely no idea who I was.

"So," I said to you.

"So."

"What's up?"

You laughed. Inane question, I know. But I was trying to show that I could be receptive to whatever you threw my way. I stared at you. Wanting you to know I meant it.

"I'm lonely," you said.

That stung. Just a little. You were sitting with me. We were close enough so that my hand grazed yours when I reached for the sugar.

You sighed. "I just miss him so much. I didn't know I could miss someone this way. I'm just . . . It's just . . . I have this vast emptiness inside me. And I know that might sound crazy, because we haven't even been together all that long, but now we are, and my life has changed, and I can't even remember what anything was like before, and it's as if I need him to breathe. He's *everything* to me. And I'm everything to him. And don't look at me that way, Nell. Seriously, don't."

I tried to neutralize my face. Slacken every muscle. "Like what?"

"Like that." You pointed at me and squinted. "Like Mom morphed with an abused puppy."

"Layla."

"Don't."

"Don't what?"

"Don't judge me. And don't make this about you. This is not about you. It's about me."

"Layla."

"What?"

"I don't know. Just . . . give me a minute here. Okay?" I didn't like hearing you sound desperate. Needy. Irrational. Was this what it meant to be in *real love*?

"You've got thirty seconds."

I stirred my latte with my pinky. "Wow."

"I know. It's crazy. But it's also a-*mazing*."

"I'm happy for you, I guess."

"Thanks, Nell."

"I don't know what else to say."

You reached across the table and took me by the hand. "You don't need to say anything else. It means a lot that you can be happy for me."

I didn't point out that I'd said I'm happy for you, *I guess.*

But you looked ecstatic, actually. So how could I not be happy for you?

The waiter who didn't recognize me circled back. "How are we doing over here, ladies? Got everything you need?"

"We've got it all," you said. "We're living the dream."

He laughed. "Sure looks like it."

That's maybe the moment, more than any other, when I realized that though we're close in age, though we share the same DNA, the world sees us differently. Especially the world of men.

You looked out the window and smiled. "Everyone thinks they know him, but they don't. I know him. Truly. Do you want to know what he wrote in my book?"

"Sure."

"He wrote: *To YOU. Love ME.* That's who we are to each other. We are the you and the me. It's simple. He's just . . ." A sigh. "He's not like anybody else."

"Nobody is like anybody else."

"You're like me."

I knew what you were doing, but still, I liked hearing it. Yes, you are like me. I am like you.

"Go on. . . ."

"He's, like, open and unafraid to articulate his feelings. He treats me better than anybody ever has. Do you know any boys who can tell you how they feel, really tell you how they feel?"

"Felix."

"That's different. Felix is your friend. I mean, look around you." I looked around. You slapped my wrist. "Not literally.

Like, think of the boys at school. Do you notice how they are with their girlfriends, if they even have girlfriends? Love is pretty much dead in high school."

I thought of Hugh Feldman giving Ava Price the play's sole standing ovation. I even thought of Sam telling me the view looked better with me in his window. You were being ridiculous.

But I clung to Duncan's words. *Start being a better sister.*

We ordered a second round of lattes and you talked. And talked and talked and talked. At first you thought you just had a crush. A crush like so many girls before you. But then you felt the connection. The way he looked at you when you spoke. He saw through your art, understood you in ways you didn't yet understand yourself. Two people are strangers to each other and then, suddenly, they are not. All at once you knew him. And he knew you. And you felt as if your whole life had been leading up to knowing this person.

Did I understand? *Could* I understand?

We took our conversation outside, found ourselves in Golden Gate Park at Children's Playground. We sat on a bench and you talked. And talked and talked and talked. And as you talked I felt some part of myself recharging. Like the way certain species of animal can regenerate a piece of · themselves they've lost—a fin, a tail, a skin. I started to feel like me again, and damn, Layla, if it didn't feel great being your trusted ally. Your confidante. Closer than close, only seventeen months apart. *Nellayla.*

A surprise December sun warmed the tops of our heads.

We watched as a line of kids dragged flattened cardboard boxes up to the top of the rock slide and flew down at dangerous speeds. I was always afraid of that slide.

You nudged me and said, "I think it's time."

I reached into the pocket of my jacket to check the clock on my phone (and, yes, to see if Sam had returned my text).

"Mrs. Literal." You took the phone from my hands. "I mean grab some cardboard. It's time you go for it."

"No thanks."

"Why not?"

"Oh, I don't know . . . maybe the risk of permanent brain damage?"

"Come on. Let's breathe some life into this vacation. If we can't go away, let's go back and do all the things we used to do, that we don't do anymore because we think we're too old."

"But I never went down that slide."

"True." You pushed me until I rose from the bench. "Now's your chance to rewrite history."

I stood around watching until a boy with strawberry hair took pity on me and offered me his produce box from Andronico's.

I know all this sounds as if it's building up to something, some metaphor about facing fears, taking risk, sliding toward the unknown, but honestly, it was just kind of awkward. I hit that sand and laughed like a kid.

This was the first stop on our Tour of the Places We Used to Go.

We chose a destination a day. Ghirardelli's. The Musée

Méchanique. Alcatraz. The carousel at Yerba Buena. The ice rink in Union Square.

We were kids with nothing to do but revisit a childhood that had receded far less than I'd realized. We didn't need anybody else. But more than that, we were better without anybody else.

We traversed the city by day. At night you stayed in your room, on your computer, connected to him by satellites and signals that allowed you to talk face to face. To stare into each other's eyes. To remind yourselves of the risks you were taking to be together. At least, that was what you told me each morning. That he said he missed you. He loved you. *Your eyes,* he'd say. *God, I love your eyes.*

As my text to Sam sat somewhere in technology purgatory, I decided you were right. Love *is* dead in high school. It was dead for me. Forget a face-to-face connection; Sam couldn't even be bothered to text back a *K* or a *thx* or even a ☺.

The more you told me about the things Mr. B. said to you (he quoted poetry!), the more the few kind things Sam said to me began to fade, and all I could remember was that lime-in-the-teeth high five. The way he called *later.* Would there be a *later* for Sam and me? It didn't feel like it.

You tried your best to share your optimistic outlook on love. To rub some of it off onto me and my hopeless situation. There was the comment you made about how Sam probably left his phone home to avoid the roaming charges, but also you told me to be patient.

I remember we were standing out at the tip of the Wave Organ, surrounded by water. I've always loved the Wave

Organ, the way that collection of rock and pipe responds to the changing tide in the bay. Sometimes the sounds are subtle, sometimes cacophonous. That day the water lapped gently and the music it created was almost like what you hear in a creepy movie when someone is lurking right around the corner.

"High school boys don't know how to handle real emotion or connection," you said. "Just because he hasn't contacted you doesn't mean he isn't thinking about you. He probably doesn't even know what he's feeling yet. Just wait."

That was my favorite day. My favorite stop on our tour. Despite the ominous music of the Wave Organ, despite that warning, I saw a happy ending.

Do you remember that day? How it felt to stand out at that rocky tip with me? Us, in isolation. Us, together. We had a good time that day, didn't we?

I hope, Layla. I pray, even though you know how I feel about religion, that this wasn't our last good time.

FELIX CALLED ME ON HIS way back from the airport.

"I know school starts tomorrow, and I know how you need your beauty rest, but wanna sneak out for a donut?"

"The one thing I don't need is a donut." Not after all the sweets on our Tour of the Places We Used to Go. "Just come over. I'm at my mom's."

"I'll be there in an hour."

"Great."

"I'm just warning you, I look hot. Seriously hot. My homeland agrees with me."

"I'm bracing myself."

I didn't want school to start again, but I was happy to have Felix back. And happy to see Mom. I missed her, and the part of me that lived with her. Not only the way we were together, but my room there, the kitchen, the streets, that particular patch of city. It was like I'd been favoring one leg over the other—and it was nice to get my balance back.

I'd convinced myself that things would be different when we went back to school. That you could live equally in the Mr. B. world and the regular world. I believed you were happy. That you weren't ruining your life or making an unspeakably bad mistake. That your secret was one I should keep. Those two timeless winter weeks had cast a spell on me.

Felix did look great. Sun-kissed with shaggier hair and even the slightest hint of man stubble. He smelled like coconut.

He hugged me for a very long time.

"I'm sorry," he said. I was the one who owed the apology. I'd been a brat. Boy-crazy and a little bitchy.

"Please," I told Felix. "I'm the one who's sorry."

"But I—"

I kissed his cheek, feeling the soft prickle of his first beard. "I'm sorry, Felix. Really sorry."

We went out to the square of yard behind Mom's house. We took blankets and sat in the reclining chairs she'd bought for sunbathing—an opportunity that presents itself once every two years. The sky was dark and fogless.

"How's Angel?"

"The surgery's next Monday."

"Good."

"Yeah."

Mom broke the silence that followed when she leaned out the window above. "Hot cocoa, anyone?"

"I'll take a whiskey," Felix answered.

"Cocoa it is, then."

She came down carrying a tray with a teapot and two cups. She shot me the evil eye when she saw the blankets I'd taken outside. There were indoor blankets and outdoor blankets. But she didn't want to scold me in front of Felix. She's got such a Mom crush on him.

"So," Felix said. "Tell me everything."

"I missed you." This was both true and false at the same time.

"And Sam?"

"What about Sam?"

"Did you miss him too or did you spend your whole break with his tongue down your throat?"

"Jesus, Felix."

"It's *Hey-soos*. Don't go forgetting your Spanish."

"Sam was away."

"Where'd he go?"

I couldn't admit that I didn't know.

"It doesn't matter."

There were so many things I wanted to say to Felix that night, but instead I stretched out on the sun chair in the dark and listened as he tried to talk himself out of being afraid of Angel's operation. I stroked his arm. I refilled his cup with lukewarm cocoa. I tried not to think about the next morning, walking down the hall and into Sam. It would no longer be just you and me, better without anybody else.

Eventually Felix got up to leave, though I wished he never would. I thought of him that first day of school, standing on the sidewalk with his ridiculous flat-brimmed baseball cap and eager grin.

"Will you wait for me? Out front?"

He cocked his head. "Of course."

"Thanks, Felix."

"De nada."

I imagined many different ways my reunion with Sam might go, from a high five to a quick hug to a grand embrace where he held me, dipped me back, and kissed me long and deep. Patience, I thought. He's sorting out his feelings. What I didn't imagine was a barely perceptible nod. And when I say barely perceptible, I mean that I may have made it up.

I tried to construct an alternate narrative:

Maybe he didn't see me and that wasn't a nod in my direction but at someone else behind me.

Maybe he was waiting for me to give him a high five or quick hug and when I kept walking I hurt his feelings.

Maybe he saw me but he didn't say anything because there was a note waiting for me in my locker, about how he missed me and wanted to kiss me again.

The verdict was in by the end of the day, delivered by Felix: "Sam Fitzpayne is a total dick."

"What?"

"Sam Fitzpayne is a total dick. A cock. A prick. A wiener. Do I need to make it more clear?"

"That'll do." I felt nauseous. I didn't want to hear what Felix had to say next, although, on some level, I already knew. Sam had walked by me in the hall. He didn't cross the cafeteria at lunch to say hello. And there were the glances from random people all day long. I don't mean to sound paranoid, but I know when people are staring at me.

And you. Before all that happened, before that night in his room and your words of encouragement that followed, you'd warned me. You'd told me there was something about Sam you didn't trust. A *cruelness,* you'd said. I hated that you understood more about everything than me.

Felix waited for me on a bench across the street from school, working up his list of names for Sam. He waved me over and I took my time crossing at the light.

School had let out. With no soccer or play rehearsal I didn't feel free, just lost. I'd wanted to find you. Maybe walk the miles home instead of braving the bus. I'd even checked the art room, but the lights were out and the door was locked.

"Should we go get a coffee so I can expound?" He looked up at me, shielding his eyes from the sun. "Tell you all the ways he is so very penislike?"

I thought about the afternoon we'd spent at the café drinking lattes, and the waiter with the smile he reserved just for you. I didn't want to go back there. Maybe ever.

"No. Just give it to me straight." I sat down next to him.

"Sam shot his mouth off about what happened at his party. With you. Upstairs. He told anyone who'd listen."

Maybe this sounds perverse, but my first reaction was delight. My logic trapped someplace between *He remembered!* and *He's not embarrassed!* But of course I know there's talking and there's *talking.* There's telling and there's *telling.*

"The worst part is, it's like . . . he doesn't even realize you're my best friend. How could he not bother noticing that?" He shook his head. "If he didn't outweigh me by twenty-five pounds, I'd have punched him in his preternaturally good-looking face."

I looked down at my feet. My mind in overdrive, like that little spinning rainbow wheel you get on the computer. Searching for some way this would all be okay.

I could feel Felix staring at me.

"You're not saying anything."

I shrugged.

"Why did you do it?" he asked quietly. "I mean, I'm not, like, mad, or judging you or anything, but why did you have sex with Sam Fitzpayne?"

"What?"

"You hardly knew him."

I stood up and starting walking toward the park. Then jogging. Then running.

"Nell!" Felix shouted.

I didn't turn to see if he was coming after me, though I must have known he would.

I scrambled through the thick ivy to the jogging trail that wound through the woods. I could hear shouting and laughter coming from the playground in the distance. Kids with their flimsy cardboard squares shooting down that goddamn rock slide. The path spilled out onto the back of a baseball diamond. I kept going. Not looking back. I finally lost steam around the soccer fields, hurled my backpack to the ground, and collapsed on the grass. Felix joined me, planted his head between his knees, and tried to catch his breath.

"Meanie. You know I'm out of shape. I'm not a jock like you."

"You didn't have to follow me." I struggled with my breath too. "And I didn't have sex with Sam."

He leaned backward into the goal and stretched out his legs. I lay down next to him. The net divided the sky above us into perfect little squares.

"You don't know how much I want that to be true."

"It is true, Felix."

He propped up his head and turned over onto his side, facing me.

"Really?"

"Really."

Felix stared at me. "I'm going to kill him."

"That might be a little extreme." I liked the way I sounded. Nonchalant. Able to crack a joke. Inside, a sick storm blew mercilessly.

"So nothing happened?" he asked. "You were up there for a pretty long time."

I thought about pressing myself against that cold window. The view of the bridge. The twinkling lights.

"I didn't say nothing happened. I just said I didn't have sex with him."

How did you feel, Layla? When you knew people were talking about you? Staring at you? Whispering your name?

You would say—you did say—that you didn't care. That you didn't give a crap. And maybe it's because what they said about you, what they thought about you as they stared at you in the hall, it was true.

But for me it was all lies. And I cared. I gave a crap. I couldn't help it.

I guess it's not fair that this was the moment the vacation spell began to lift. You probably think it's because of what Sam did to me. That I'm jealous you were loved while I was used—you had real love, I had nothing. Maybe you think I wanted some company in my heap of ruin, but I'd never wish for that.

It's just that I started to wonder. To look more carefully at the perfect picture you'd painted.

It's like that quote you parroted at me. *Everything we hear is an opinion, not a fact. Everything we see is a perspective, not the truth.*

Your version of what was happening with Mr. B. was your opinion, Layla. Your perspective, one I was able to share for those fleeting weeks, because you are a master at getting me to see things your way. Through your eyes.

But as we reentered the world, I began to do what City Day was supposed to teach me.

I began to think for myself.

THE NEXT FEW DAYS were hellish.

You probably heard the sobbing I saved for the night, my bedroom door latched. I cried until my eyes felt like leather.

He's just a boy, Duncan said. *He can't be worth all this.*

Parker tried too. *I guarantee he doesn't even know he's hurt you. He doesn't understand his power. That's the thing about beautiful boys. They don't know. They don't understand.*

The Creed brothers never would have done something like this to me. Never.

They looked at each other and shrugged. *We barely knew you.*

They weren't making me feel any better.

You knocked. "Nell?"

I sat still. The room emptied. I couldn't even hear my own breath.

"Nell?"

There was no use fighting it. You know how to make me unlock doors.

"What's wrong?"

"You don't know?"

"If I knew, I wouldn't be asking."

"How can you possibly not know?"

"Is this some sort of trick question?"

I climbed back into bed and grabbed hold of my elephant, my last remaining stuffed animal. Cupcake. Honey. Maisy. Rufus. Violet. Bob. Its name and gender had changed many times over the years.

"Sam told everyone, *everyone,* that I had sex with him."

"He didn't tell me."

"Well, I guess you're the only one he didn't tell. And you must be deaf to gossip."

You sat down on the bed's edge. "I told you I didn't trust Sam. And I don't pay attention to what people say at school."

"I didn't . . ." I buried my face in my nameless, genderless elephant. "I didn't have sex with Sam."

"I know you didn't."

"How do you know?"

"Because I know you wouldn't."

Layla, I could see that you were trying to comfort me, but this made it so much worse. How different we'd become: You could. I wouldn't. And why wouldn't I? Because I'm so much less mature than you? Because I don't know how to find real love?

"This is exactly why I steer clear of high school boys," you said.

What happened to *be patient*? What happened to *he doesn't know what he's feeling yet*? You'd said all that only to get me on your side. To win my allegiance. And now you were judging me. You would never . . . You steer clear . . . Your life was so perfect. You had all the answers in that pretty head.

She has a good head on her shoulders.

I wiped my face on my comforter.

"You really think Mr. B. is the answer? A teacher? An adult?"

"I know he is."

"What about the others?"

"What others?"

"Hazel Porter? Yelli Rothman?"

"He was never with either of them. Never. Those were rumors. He's never been with a student before. I swear it."

Oh, Layla. I know that voice. The way we sound when we're trying to convince ourselves of something we know isn't true. As Shakespeare might say: *the lady doth protest too much.*

Yes, I was angry. And yes, I suppose I wanted to hurt you in that moment. But actually, I do believe that you are the first student, the one who made him cross the line. How do I know this? I don't really, but I just believe that if the rumors about either Hazel or Yelli were true, there would have been some collateral damage. I guess in that way, I'm still a child. I believe that grown-ups get punished when they do something wrong. And I believe that if those girls had been

162

like you, desperately clinging to the conviction that it was real love, an ending wouldn't have come gently. There would have been a reckoning. Everyone would have known.

"Nell," you were pleading. For what, I wasn't sure. "He loves me. I am the only one. What we have . . . it's forever."

I could see your future, Layla, and it wasn't pretty. I didn't even need your palm. There was no way through this. He'd crossed that line for you and now there was no good end. You were in too deep.

"What's happening with you and Mr. Barr—it's not right."

"What?"

"It's not normal. It's wrong."

You stood up and backed away.

"Look, Nell, I get that you're upset. I get that Sam Fitz-payne is an asshole. I as much as told you he was. But this has nothing to do with me or my life."

"It's wrong, Layla. He's an adult. A teacher! You're a kid. You're seventeen."

"You're not thinking clearly."

"You're the one who's not thinking clearly. If you were, you wouldn't be doing this."

"I thought you understood." Your eyes burned wild.

"I want to understand, I do, but look at you. You're pan-icking. Layla, you don't panic."

"One guy screws you over and suddenly you're an ex-pert at relationships. Of course Sam dumped you. You don't understand anything. You're a baby." You turned toward my door, showing me your back. Your short shorts and skimpy tank top.

"Not true." My voice cracked.

"Stay out of my life."

The first thing I did the next morning was go to the registrar's office. Since we were only a few days into the second semester, I was allowed to drop or add nonmandatory classes. The only reasons I'd continued on in Visual Arts were because I got an A first semester (being your sister has its privileges) and also, Felix had transferred into my section.

I dropped it and added Music Appreciation.

Ms. Bellweather, the school registrar, squinted at my form. "I don't think I've ever had a student drop one of Mr. Barr's classes. Usually they fight tooth and nail to get in."

I shrugged. "I like music."

"Who doesn't? But Mr. B. could be teaching chemistry. Or Latin. Kids would still line up to take his classes." She winked at me. "Especially the girls."

Can I just say: *ewwww.*

Felix was equally confounded when I told him over lunch. "Why are you doing this?"

"I like music."

"Shut up."

"I do."

"Mr. B.'s class kicks ass. *He* kicks ass."

"Whatever. He's overrated. And his class is lame."

"Is this about Layla and the rumors? I told you those rumors always happen. Occupational hazard. They're never true."

It took all my willpower not to tell him he was wrong. "Can't I just have my own opinion? Sorry I haven't drunk the Kool-Aid like you and everybody else."

"Did you have Frosted Grumpy Flakes for breakfast?"

"No."

"Captain Cranky Crunch?"

I rolled my eyes and sighed irritably. Then I tried to smile at him. It wasn't his fault. He didn't know that I'd started to draw a new line.

That night Mom took us out for dinner. Sushi, which meant: big news. Probably that she'd met someone she thought had potential.

Despite Mom's rules about no texting at dinner, you kept your phone in your pocket and continued to check it every few minutes in a way I'm sure you thought was stealthy. Mom would have called you out on it if she hadn't been feeling so jovial.

With the arrival of our unagi rolls, you checked again. Your eyes widened.

Mom was in the middle of telling us about him—a venture capitalist, shorter than she usually goes for but still had his hair—when you interrupted.

"You dropped Visual Arts?"

"Yeah. So?" I glared. *Do you really want to do this now?*

"You dropped art, sweetie? But you're so talented."

Mom thinks we're good at everything.

"Yeah, I dropped Visual Arts. I don't like Mr. Barr. I think he's a dick. A cock. A prick. A wiener."

Mom slapped my wrist playfully. This new guy had

definitely sanded off some of her edge. "Don't say that. It's crude. I thought you loved Mr. Barr."

"Me?"

I know how you were looking at me, but I kept my eyes on Mom. I wasn't going to wilt under your glare.

"Isn't he everyone's favorite teacher?"

"Not mine."

When we got up to leave the restaurant, you grabbed my arm and pinched me hard.

"Ow!"

"What?" Mom asked.

"Layla pinched me."

Mom laughed and patted me on the back. "You girls."

Somehow I made it through the week without seeing Sam. I did everything in my power to avoid him, and clearly he made no effort to find me. People still stared. Still whispered. I imagined confronting him, grabbing him hard at his shoulders. Calling him a liar. A coward. But I didn't. Of course I didn't. That's not who I am. That's not how these stories go. I just kept my head down and tried to put the whole mess behind me. I told myself it didn't matter. *He* didn't matter.

I decamped to Felix's Saturday night. We had the place to ourselves. Angel and Julia had gone to Napa for their twentieth anniversary. Two days before his surgery.

Though I'd always envied Felix his parents' happy marriage, I never envied his lack of a sibling. I wondered if he didn't feel left out, lonely, sometimes.

We watched *Family Guy* reruns and I just enjoyed the feeling of being with someone safe. Someone who *mattered*. Who had my best interests at heart. Who wasn't testing my limits. Someone with whom I could split a six-pack of Mike's Hard Lemonade.

"You don't mind spending the evening with City Day's resident slut?" I asked.

"If only that were true."

I threw a pillow at him. "Seriously, wouldn't you rather be with someone else? Like that girl Andie from the cafeteria?"

He shrugged. "Not really."

"Why?" I was fishing, for sure. Feeling a little low. And a little drunk.

"Because, she may be cute and everything, but I love you."

"Shut up, Felix."

My phone rang. When I saw it was you, I picked it up and took it outside onto the back deck.

"Yeah?"

"Thanks a lot."

"What?"

"Now George is totally freaking out."

"About?"

"About how you dropped his class. And how you told me things between us are wrong. And he's freaked out that you know about us, because I hadn't even told him I'd told you, but then I had to tell him after you dropped the class, and now he's worried you're going to do something stupid, and he said we need to think things over. That's what he said. *We need to think things over.* And that's not good."

"Thinking isn't good?"

"Don't be a smart-ass."

Felix peeked his head out the door and shot me a *You okay?* look. I waved him back inside.

"Look, Layla . . ."

"You sound weird," you said.

"*You* sound weird." I tried not to slur my words but I was failing.

"You're drunk."

"So?"

"I blame you," you said.

"For what?"

"No, I blame *me*. This is all my fault. I never should have told you anything. I never should have trusted you."

"You can trust me, Layla."

"Obviously, I can't."

"Yes, you can. But you can't count on me to tell you something is right when I think it's wrong."

"Yeah, well, it probably wasn't right for you to sleep with Sam Fitzpayne."

"I didn't."

"That's not what people say."

I felt the sting of tears, and I could hear you trying to stifle yours on the other end of the line.

There was a long silence. We'd never had a fight like this one.

"I'm sorry," you said. I know I was supposed to say that too, but I wasn't. I hadn't done anything but drop a class with someone whose face, cool clothes, and stupid tattoo I couldn't bear to look at.

"I have to go."

"He's freaking out," you said. "And now I'm freaking out. He wouldn't even see me this weekend. He said we need to think things over. I don't have any thinking to do. I just need him."

"Take a deep breath."

"Can you come home? *Please?* I'm really freaking out."

Much as I felt the magnetic pull of your desire, I knew that it wasn't me you really wanted. I didn't like the way you sounded—so desperate—yet there was the matter of those three bottles of Mike's Hard Lemonade and Dad's impeccable nose.

"I'm staying here tonight. I'll be back tomorrow. We can talk then. Promise."

We hung up and I went back inside. Felix was in the kitchen sulking and drinking a beer. The hard lemonade was all gone.

"Who was that?"

"Layla."

"Yeah, sure."

"What?"

"If it was Layla, why'd you have to take the phone outside?"

I snatched the bottle from his hands and took a long swig even though I hate the taste of beer. "Who'd you think it was?"

He shrugged.

"Felix?"

"What? Okay, so I thought it was Sam, the way you snuck outside and all. The whispering and whatever. Anyway . . .

I just don't want you letting him off the hook. I don't want him using his charms to weasel his way back into your life."

"That wasn't Sam. You know Sam doesn't call me. Ever. He can't weasel his way back into my life because he was never in my life in the first place. Sam doesn't care about me. Sam used me. Sam humiliated me. Sam lied about me. Sam . . ."

I started to cry. Felix stood up and took me in his arms. I wept into his T-shirt. He smoothed my hair. He whispered in my ear: *shh shh shh.* And then he lifted my face, and he looked at me, and I knew.

Felix De La Cruz was going to kiss me.

I jumped back.

"Hey!"

"What?"

"What was that?"

"What was what?"

"That." I gestured back and forth between us.

"Nell."

"What?"

"Nell . . ." He looked down at his shoes. "I love you."

"I love you too."

"No, I mean, I think I *love you,* love you."

"Felix, you're drunk."

"Yes, I am."

"So c'mon. Don't do this."

He went and sat back down at the counter and cradled his beer in his hands. He took a long pull. I stared at him.

"Felix, I—"

"It's okay. Don't worry. This doesn't have to become one of those horrible, painfully awkward moments that we pretend never happened but think about every time we look at each other. It doesn't have to change anything between us. Deal?"

I nodded.

"It's just . . . I don't know. Like, I look at my dad and my mom, you know? What they have. They're best friends. Who doesn't want that? And yeah, I'm young, and yeah, I think about sex, like, all the time, and I look around me and there are all these cute girls. And it's not like I think that right now I need what my dad and mom have or anything. I'm just in high school."

He finished his beer.

"But the thing is: What if I don't have a lot of time left? I'm . . . my father's son. I have an adrenal cortex just like him. What if mine gets tumors on it too? What if I only have one chance? Wouldn't I want to make the most of that? And if I only have one chance"—he locked his eyes on mine— "I really want that chance to be with you."

"Felix." I took a tentative step toward him. "You aren't sick. Except maybe in the head. You're young and healthy." I wanted to add—*and beautiful.*

He is. He's a beautiful boy.

He put his head down on the counter and groaned. I went over and rubbed his back. I thought I knew every inch of Felix, but there was so much I'd never bothered to notice.

"I'm scared," he said. "I'm really, really scared."

"I am too."

That night we slept in his parents' room, in their enormous bed. We drifted off at distant ends of the mattress, watching some loud, violent movie.

But in sleep I'd moved to his side and I woke in the morning with my head on his shoulder, because that's the way it is.

We always find each other.

WHEN I GOT BACK TO Dad's in the morning, he cornered me in the kitchen.

"What's up with her?" He gestured toward your closed door. "She's been holed up in there since yesterday. She won't come out. Not even with the promise of pancakes."

"Dad, your pancakes taste like butt sweat."

He smiled briefly, then turned serious. "What's wrong? You must know."

My blood pounded a frantic rhythm in my ears:

This. Is. It.

Tell. Him. Now.

This. Is. It.

Tell. Him. Now.

Remember how much you hated Sonia at the beginning? Scowling and sulking whenever she came around? And remember how I'd always go and sit near her and show her my drawings or ask her about her cat or whatever? I didn't like her back then either, but I didn't want to make Dad feel bad. Layla: in addition to being the keeper of your secrets, I am the keeper of the peace in our family. I don't cause the ripples, I'm the one who smooths them over. I don't know how to do things any other way.

"Just girl stuff, Dad. She'll be okay."

Later, at Mom's, you told me he wanted to end things. He said the risk was too great. He thought you understood that nobody could ever know, but then you'd gone and told me.

"Oh God, why did I tell you?" you wailed.

Because our lives are intertwined.

"Layla, how could you expect to be in a relationship 'forever' and never tell anyone about it? That's insanity."

You buried your face in your pillow. "I should never have told you. Never. I should never have told you. And now . . . it's over."

I hope you believe that I hated seeing you hurt like that. I hated the desperate you. The way you wore your heartache.

But.

I could feel things getting right again.

I kept thinking of that Emily Dickinson poem, as weird as that may sound, but as you finally cried yourself to sleep in my bed too small for the two of us, the title came to me: "After a great pain, a formal feeling comes."

I lay there, listening to you breathe, and I felt a calmness.

A settling of pieces back into their natural places. Just you. Just me.

The way it's meant to be.

Relationships are a mystery to me. I'm sure you'd say it's because I've never been in one. But anyway, I didn't know that you can fight bitterly, swear that it's over, cry yourself to sleep in your sister's bed on Sunday, and then return to each other Monday morning.

You weren't in school. Neither was he.

I should have known that an ending wouldn't come so simply.

Felix wasn't in school either because he was at the hospital waiting for his father to come out of surgery.

Around fourth period it finally occurred to me that if there was a wrong place to be, I was sitting in its epicenter. What was I doing in Spanish without Felix? What was I doing in school without you? Why was I expected to live my life by the rules when nobody else seemed to?

"Perdon," I said as I stood. I didn't wait for permission; I gathered my things, shoved them into my backpack, and left school.

I hailed a taxi. I'd never taken a cab alone. I felt pulled in two directions but said, "California Pacific Medical Center, please."

Felix and Julia sat in the waiting room on the fifth floor. Though it was noon, in the middle of a school day, neither seemed surprised to see me rush in. Julia hugged me and quickly sat back down. Hands folded in her lap, eyes straight ahead, as if only her stillness would ensure the desired outcome.

Felix took me by the hand. "Thank you for coming here and bailing on school. I know how that goes against your inner nerd."

I kissed him. On the lips. Just a little. Like a friend. Like I'd done many times before.

But his lips. They were soft. Like silk. Like silk that tastes like candy. Like candy that tastes of rosewater and sugar. Like . . . Turkish Delight.

Weird, right?

How could I have been thinking all this in the midst of everything else?

Maybe this moment, me standing in a Pepto-Bismol-pink hospital waiting room thinking about Felix's lips while you'd ditched school to be with your teacher—maybe this was the true epicenter of all that was wrong.

All I could glean from Julia's conversation with the young doctor in blue scrubs is that the surgery went well and Angel had a decent chance, a solid mathematical chance. She held Felix and wept.

I drank burned coffee with them in the hospital cafeteria before heading home. By the time I arrived it was six o'clock, Mom was waiting for me, and she was pissed.

The school called her at work to inform her that Layla had disappeared after first period and that I'd just stood up and walked out in the middle of Spanish. What was going on? I could almost hear Ms. Bellweather's slight Southern drawl. Something wrong at home? Were we both felled by the same illness? Was this some sort of protest by the Golden sisters?

Mom does not like getting caught off guard. She's way too much of a control freak.

"I've texted you both," she said to me, a vodka tonic in her hand. "Since neither of you bothered to respond, you can say good-bye to your precious cell phones for at least a week."

"Mom."

"Where is your sister?"

"I don't know."

"I don't believe you."

I couldn't help it; my face flushed immediately. I'm a lousy liar. I pulled off my jacket. I was sweating despite the chill in the kitchen.

"I can tell you where I went if you have any interest in that." I dropped my stuff on the floor. She was already so mad I figured it made little difference.

"Don't talk to me like that," she said as she picked up my things and threw them into the front hallway closet.

"I was at the hospital."

I let that sit there, enjoying my moment of superiority. Mom gestured for me to go on.

"I was with Felix and Julia while Angel was having his adrenal glands removed."

"You can't just leave school without permission."

"I thought the circumstances were extenuating."

"And Layla?"

"I already told you I have no idea where she is."

"So it's pure coincidence? You and your sister ditching school on the same day?"

The sound of your key rattling the front lock followed. You called out, *"Helllooooooooo?"* in a way only someone who had no idea she'd been busted could. I guess it made sense that you hadn't checked your phone. The only time you cared who was calling or texting you was when you weren't with *him*.

"What?" you said when you saw Mom's face.

"Where were you?" she asked.

You looked over at me with a startling fierceness. "What did she tell you?" The *she* dripping with venom.

"She didn't tell me anything," Mom said. "She told me she had no idea where you were, which is something I find very hard to believe."

She keeps your secrets! *She* protects you! *She* doesn't want you looking at her that way. But . . . *she* wishes *she* could tell Mom or Dad or somebody.

"Well," you said, hanging up your jacket and putting away your backpack. "I wasn't feeling good. You know, cramps and stuff. And I went by the nurse's office but nobody was there, so I decided to go to Walgreens to get some Advil, but it was like, *really* bad, so I took the Advil and I was walking back to school, but like, my lower back was totally killing me and I just couldn't imagine sitting in class without wanting to die, and I passed one of those foot massage places? You know, the ones that are like twenty bucks for an hour? And I know I shouldn't have, but I was feeling so crappy, and I went in and they have these crazy comfortable chairs and I sat down and paid for ninety minutes, and the Advil finally kicked in and I felt, like, so much better. So then I went back to school, but my last class was PE, and even though I felt better I wasn't up for PE, so I just went to the library and spent the rest of the afternoon there. I finished my history paper. That's the good news. It isn't even due for another week but I think it's, like, in really good shape."

"What about my texts?" Mom said.

"Oh." You shrugged. "I left my phone at home."

Mom let out a sigh. She looked at me, searching for a nod, something to let her know she wasn't crazy to believe your long, rambling explanation. I gave her that nod.

You kissed her cheek. "What's for dinner? I'm starving."

Over bowls of spaghetti with garlic and butter Mom delivered a lecture about how we still need to do things by the book even if what we're doing isn't wrong, because rules give order to society and it's our tacit obligation as members of society to live by those rules.

In other words: don't leave school without permission.

She didn't take away our phones.

After dinner you suggested we go for ice cream. Mom took a pass. You knew she'd take a pass because she's forever dieting despite having a pretty impressive figure for a woman pushing sixty. We grabbed our jackets and headed over to Chestnut Street.

"I can't believe we both ditched on the same day." You said this like it was funny. High five. Aren't we awesome?

"Yeah."

"So how's Felix?"

I wanted to say something about the realignment that had started to happen. About how he almost kissed me and it hadn't become one of those horrible, painfully awkward moments we pretend never happened. It became something I couldn't forget, a moment I relived again and again.

"He's okay. His dad's surgery went well. Everyone seems optimistic."

"That's great. Just great."

Uh-oh.

"I was with George today," you continued.

"And?"

"And we're working things out."

"Layla."

"Nell. Be happy for me. I love him. I don't want to be without him. I can't be without him."

"What changed?"

"Nothing *changed,* Nell," you said with the tone of a frustrated preschool teacher. "It's just that I helped him realize that what we have may be hard, and it may be work, and it may seem wrong to people on the outside, but it's worth fighting for."

We walked past what once was a soap store before it became Madam Mai's palmistry shop. Now it's a jeweler's specializing in seriously hideous necklaces. Do you think this is what Madam Mai meant when she predicted your love-filled future before skipping out on her rent?

If she were still here, if we could part her velvet curtains and enter her reading room, I think she'd take you by the collar with her tiny hands and shake you, yelling: *No! This not Madam Mai's fortune! You make big mistake!*

We walked past the ice cream place. You never wanted ice cream. I let you go on for a few blocks about how much better you were feeling, how everyone experiences a rough patch, how grateful you were that I was there for you in your despair, but that I shouldn't hold that against George, he'd just had cold feet.

You told me I couldn't tell anyone. Ever. Did I understand?

I understood.

But a piece was missing. I could feel it. I could smell it with my Goldenian nose. I just couldn't see it.

"He broke up with you," I said. "He said it was too risky. Too much was at stake . . . and then he left school with you? In the middle of the morning? What happened?"

You laughed. "Nothing happened. He loves me. That's all."

That night the Creeds were all fired up.

What is it? they asked. *What did she do? How did she get him to leave school with her? She must have said something. She must have done something.*

They wouldn't give up. *What is it? What could it be? What did she do? You're her sister. You must know.*

I didn't.

You always do. That's what it means to be the younger sister. You know. You know everything.

I put a pillow over my head. I wanted to go to sleep. No use. I could feel them, waiting. Waiting for me to do something.

I WISH I COULD HAVE let it go. Believed that you were happy, that it was right, that it would all turn out okay. But I know you better than anybody else. Better even than Mom and Dad. Why couldn't they see it?

You weren't you.

I don't care what Mr. B. wrote in that stupid Rothko book: *To YOU. Love ME.* I know the YOU, because I am the ME. And, Layla, the YOU with him is not the real *you*.

No, you weren't sobbing in my bed anymore. You were back to *Everything Is Awesome and Life Is Amazing* Layla. But now I understood the delicate barrier that kept the sobbing you at bay.

I thought of that fortune. The one I keep in my wallet: *With time and patience the mulberry leaf becomes the silk gown.* You are the silk gown. The fragile silk gown.

It's always suited Mom and Dad best to think of us as smart and mature young women with good sense who make good choices so that they could wrap themselves up in their own lives and fall asleep a little on the job of being our parents. All these years, Layla, we've tried to make things easy on them. We go back and forth, back and forth, smart and mature, building a bridge between two lives and crossing it over and over again. You know I've always hated being called a baby, but I started to wish it were true. The baby of whom nothing is asked or expected.

I wanted to go to them, to tell them, to put them in charge, but I didn't know how. I was afraid to cause that earthquake.

I think we all fall back into our patterns. Play our parts when we don't know what else to do. So as you went back to Layla, the girl with the world on a string, I went back to playing Nell, adoring sister, keeper of the peace.

The sister who lies for you.

I lied to Mom when you told her you were going to the park after school to kick a soccer ball around with some of the girls from the team. I lied to Dad when you told him you were tagging along with Felix and me to the Animation Festival at the Kabuki Theater.

Felix. We never made it to the Animation Festival. We don't go anywhere these days but to his house, where I bring stacks of magazines and provisions from Happy Donuts. And while Angel rests upstairs, we sit down in the basement, where Felix doesn't try to kiss me and sometimes we don't say anything and that's okay.

I've tiptoed right up to the edge of confiding in him, but

I always step back at the last second. When I'm with him, I can almost forget about you, because I'm thinking about me and I'm thinking about him, and I know that this must be a good thing.

One day he asked.

"Is something up with Layla?" He was marking the *San Francisco* magazine I'd brought with a list of the top one hundred desserts in the city, mapping out a plan of attack. We had to eat three a week if we wanted to meet our goal of trying them all by the end of the year.

"What do you mean?"

"Well, she's kind of MIA lately. And something seems, I don't know ... different with her, or with you and her, or something."

Felix isn't Mom, and he isn't Dad, and he has his own troubles, but still, he's the only one who knew the right question to ask.

I started making a list, the top reasons it should be obvious to anyone paying attention that you were in a whole heap of trouble. 1. You skipped our girls' weekend in Big Sur. 2. You ditched school. 3. You locked yourself in your room and cried for a whole weekend. 4. You don't hang out with your friends anymore. 5. You can't shut up about a painter who only uses, like, two colors in big boring squares. 6. A new, unbridgeable gap had opened between us.

You were so careful. I always wanted the best for you, but lately I'd been wishing for you to stumble, to screw up. Hoping someone would catch you. Someone would see you together someplace. Someone, other than me, would know.

How could our parents not see?

I lied to Felix like I lied to them. *She's a junior. School is stressful. Blah, blah, blah.*

Layla, you know I'd happily lie for you to save your life, or to fix your life, but it's a different story entirely to lie about something that I believe is ruining your life.

Mr. B.

George.

I probably wouldn't ever have figured out what brought him back to you if it weren't for the Creeds. Sometimes they point me in the direction I didn't realize I needed to go.

It was another sleepless night. Sleeplessness had become my new normal. On this night I relived that morning you left school with him. Your seat in US History: empty. His classroom: dark, locked. Why? Why would he take such a risk?

Why don't you check her phone? Parker whispered.

There are things a sister just doesn't do.

She's a sound sleeper. Go for it.

I kicked off my covers. I was hot and cold at the same time. My heart raced. I stood alone in the darkness of my room. I was proud that I'd never violated your trust. I hadn't even told Felix. But reading your texts? How could I justify that?

I'm telling you about your phone when I don't even have to. I didn't find anything because you were smart enough to delete any communication with him. I couldn't even find him in your contacts. You slept, your face unsuspecting as I stood by your bedside scrolling through your history.

What's up?

Where u been?

When can we hang?

R U mad at me?

Your messages were mostly from Schuyler and Liv, trying to make sense of your disappearing act.

I put your phone back by your bedside. And then I grabbed your backpack. Heavy. That goddamn Rothko book—you took it everywhere. I lugged your bag into my room, put it in the middle of my floor, and stared at it.

It's not going to open itself.

C'mon. Get it over with.

Books. Papers. Homework. Pencils. Gum. Calculator. Lipstick. I pulled out your wallet. You kept it in the outside zippered pocket. I'd told you more than once that you should keep your wallet inside your bag where someone riding the bus with you wouldn't be able to take advantage as you texted or read, but you laughed and said, "Geez, Nell. You always imagine the worst in people."

I pulled out a picture of us, from a photo booth at Pier 39. For a second I felt profoundly happy, and then I was struck by a sickening sadness. You couldn't carry a photo of the person you loved. You couldn't keep his number in your contacts. You had to erase all signs of him. If an anthropologist stumbled upon your possessions and tried to form a narrative of your life, he'd never conclude that there was somebody essential to you. Someone you believed you could not live without.

I finally got why you took that Rothko book everywhere. See, Layla? It's not that I don't understand you. I get how hard it must have been, how sad really, to have something so enormous be your secret. I could feel it as I put my hands on your things, the power of that burden.

In your wallet, a stack of receipts. I flipped through them, not really thinking that something so insubstantial could hold the answer I was after.

The connector.

What made him decide that he couldn't break things off. What made him leave school with you instead of leaving you alone with a shattered heart.

You weren't totally lying to Mom that day. I guess that explains why your story unfurled so naturally. You did go to Walgreens. You did buy Advil.

You also bought a First Response Gold Early Digital Pregnancy Test for $15.98.

I LAY AWAKE ALL NIGHT. The sun lightened the walls and then the ceiling of my room and still, no clarity. I don't know what today will bring. What I'll do. I suppose this describes most days. There are always things we can't predict, the plot twists we don't see coming.

Layla, you are not pregnant. I believe you are not pregnant. But what really kills me is this: I know you wish you were. That's why you walked away from school that day, isn't it? You walked toward Walgreens hoping, praying for something drastic to bring him back. Something bigger than you.

Did the test come out negative? And when it did, did you cry? And then, did you alter it? Draw a little pink line where there wasn't one? Or maybe you just threw it away and then told him, with that tear-streaked face: *It's positive.*

You can lie to him, Layla, but you cannot lie to me.

We live together and we share a bathroom and we share so many other things, including our cycle, and to put it crudely, I needed a tampon last week and you'd snagged the last one.

If this is your strategy, Layla, to fool him into staying, then you've acted without thinking. Failed to see the future. Forsaken that good head on your shoulders. What will happen when he finds out you're not telling him the truth?

Or . . . maybe you were pregnant? Maybe that little pink line showed up all on its own and he took you to have an abortion.

Or . . . maybe you are pregnant? I could be wrong about whether someone who is pregnant might need a tampon. I don't know everything, Layla. There are still so many things I don't understand. So there. I've said it: you know more than me.

I'm feeling a little crazed as I spin and respin scenarios, everything distorted by sleeplessness. As the morning light continued its climb across my ceiling, I wished for a real earthquake, not a metaphoric one. I closed my eyes and tried to conjure it, the stillness just before everything changes. The ground trembling and then a roar. Everything turned upside down. Maybe then, in its aftermath, I'd find the courage to do something. I'd know what to do.

Is that prayer? I'm not sure. If it is, it seems to be going unanswered, because the earth is quiet and Mom is outside with the car running, waiting to drive us to school.

You sit up front, backpack on your lap. Why do you always get the front seat? I stare at that backpack. Black with zebra-striped straps. I returned it to your room last night. You took a quick breath, flipped over to face the wall, and settled down into sleep again.

That bag in your lap with an outside zippered pocket that contains your wallet, inside of which lives a stack of receipts—that bag is the end. The living, breathing end of what I am capable of doing for you. What secrets I can keep. That backpack is the creature on my shoulder—devil or angel, I don't know—that tells me the time has come.

"Mom," I croak from my seat in the back. She doesn't hear me over the sound of the radio. "Mom."

She reaches out and adjusts the knob. Silence. "Yes, my love?"

You turn around and look at me, searching.

In this moment, Layla, on this morning after a night of no sleep, after praying for a natural disaster, it is you and me and Mom together, safe inside her car, just the three of us, and . . . I can't tell her. I don't know how to tell her. I can't pry the words out. I can't bear to see what they will do to your searching face. I can't even figure which words they'd be—*Layla is pretending she's pregnant?* Or *Layla was pregnant and had an abortion?* Or *Layla is pregnant and she needs help?*

She needs help. Those are the words.

"Nothing," I say. Maybe you're right. I should stay out of your life. Let you make your own mistakes. Maybe it's time to start untwining us.

Even if I could tell her, I know you'd deflect, deny, derail. You'd dismiss my list of top reasons why it should be obvious to anyone paying attention and make it all my fault, my

191

crazy fantasy. Nell, always envious. Now she's turning what stupid kids at school say into some big drama. Why'd she even have to come to City Day? Why'd she have to follow me here? Why does she follow me everywhere? She's lying. She doesn't know what she's talking about. She can't prove anything.

But I *can* prove it.

I have that receipt in my pocket.

As Mom pulls the car into the drop-off lane, I think: maybe I should just go to *him,* tell *him* that he must leave you alone because he is making you do crazy, stupid things, but I know I won't. He is a teacher and I am a student. There are things I cannot do.

I can't tell Mom, and I can't confront Mr. Barr, and Dad is buried in work and we won't see him until Friday night, and this can't wait until Friday night, and anyway, any talk with Dad about sex and his daughters is inconceivable.

I go and I stand outside Ms. Bellweather's office. She's talking on the phone and drinking coffee. To her it's probably just another day. With lists of things to do. Schedules to juggle. Students to wrangle.

What if I walked in and reported him?

City Day has rules, standards, and they need to know that their teacher is violating everything sacred. They need to take a closer look at the one whose class the girls fight tooth and nail to get into. *Wink. Wink.*

She'd look up at me and in her slight Southern drawl say, "Can I help you?"

And then . . . what?

I'm standing in the hallway of this place I've come to love, and I am totally lost.

That's when I feel a hand on my shoulder.

"Nell?"

I can't speak.

"What's wrong?" Felix turns me to face him. "What's the matter?"

"I need to talk to you."

He rolls his eyes. "Nell, I told you, we don't need to do this. Can't we just forget everything? I was drunk, okay? I was an idiot. Please don't overanalyze this. Just forget about it, okay?"

"No, it's not that," I say, though I don't much like Felix blaming his confession of love on being drunk. This isn't how I see it. He's not an idiot. I don't want to forget. I want to overanalyze and then think about it some more. About him. About us.

"What, then?"

"We need to go somewhere."

He looks down the hallway at the students rushing to their classes.

He sighs. "Okay."

I wish we could go to the Bison Paddock. Sit and watch those steadfast buffalo with lives so dull the very idea that they harbor secrets makes us laugh. *Look at that one,* I'd say to Felix. *She's having an affair with her teacher, and when he tried breaking things off with her, she told him that she's pregnant. Look at that one. She was pregnant but she had an abortion and didn't tell her sister. Look at that one. . . .*

Layla, you're desperate enough to do anything to hold on to him, but I don't believe that any of this is your fault.

It's his.

He's done this to you.

We don't go to the buffalo. I don't want to leave school because I promised Mom I wouldn't. We go to the drama section of the library, the most secluded spot on campus, and we sit on the floor. Our knees touch.

"I have to tell you something," I whisper.

"Right. But I have to warn you, I'm sort of done in. It's been really hard at home. Dad is barely eating. He's so weak. I don't like being the strongest man in the house."

I think of the Einstein poster again. *The only reason for time is so that everything doesn't happen at once.* Clearly Einstein wasn't as smart as people make him out to be.

"Felix." I take his hand and squeeze it. I want him to see that I can hold both his pain and my own at the same time. And while holding our pain I can also feel the way his skin warms mine. And as I feel his warmth I think, yes, if I didn't have a lot of time left, if I only had one chance, I would want it to be with him. And it occurs to me that all of this might be what it means to be in love. Real love.

"You are the only person I can trust to tell me what to do. I don't know what to do. Oh God. I don't know what to do." I am shaking.

"Nell," he says. "I'm here. Take your time. And say whatever it is you need to say."

I take a deep breath.

SO, LAYLA, THERE'S SOMETHING I need to tell you.

Don't be mad.

Please. Please don't be mad. I hate it when you're mad at me.

I am only doing this because I love you. Because our lives are intertwined.

I've called a family meeting. Tonight. Just you and me and Mom and Dad. The original Goldens. The last time the four of us sat down together was the Christmas of my kindergarten year for *that* talk. We thought there'd be more meetings, about issues big and small. That's what Mom and Dad said, that things wouldn't change, but of course they did, because change comes even for those who don't want it.

"You have to tell them," Felix said. "They're your parents."

"I can't."

"Yes, you can." He looked at me with such intensity, I wondered if he maybe would lean over and press his lips against mine. "I know you think you have to be perfect for them, but you don't. You aren't perfect. Layla isn't perfect."

"But . . ."

"But nothing, Nell."

"But Mr. B."

"He's a Cretan."

"I thought you loved him."

He looked at me. It was a stupid thing to say. "I love *you*, Nell."

He's said this more times than I can count. Nonchalantly. Just like this. But today it means something more, or something different, and it's familiar, yet totally and completely new.

"Tell them," he says. "You have to."

Felix is right. At the end of the day, despite anything and everything else, all the changes and reincarnations, they're our parents. We're their children. They'll know how to handle it. They'll protect you. They'll help you through. That's what parents do.

They watch out for us. You can't hide your troubles from the people who watch out for you. You can't pretend your life is perfect when it's not. Just look at what happened to the Creed brothers. It's my job, Layla, to watch out for you. To help you when you need it, even if you don't know you need the help.

So I've called a family meeting.

We'll sit together, the four of us, Mom and Dad in separate chairs, we'll sit on the sofa, though I don't expect you'll drape your arm around me or *tap-tap-tap* my shoulder. I won't look at you, because that can't come to good. So I'll look ahead, at Mom, at Dad.

"What is it, honey?" they'll ask.

"What is this all about?"

And I'll say, "There's something I need to tell you."

ABOUT THE AUTHOR

Dana Reinhardt lives in San Francisco with her husband and their two daughters. She is the author of the young adult novels *A Brief Chapter in My Impossible Life, Harmless, How to Build a House, The Things a Brother Knows, The Summer I Learned to Fly,* and, for middle-grade readers, *Odessa Again.* Her books have been singled out for many awards and best of the year lists; reviewers have praised her work as "exceptional" and "funny and unforgettable." Visit her at danareinhardt.net.